8/06

EVA
UNDERGROUND

EVA UNDERGROUND

Dandi Daley Mackall

HARCOURT, INC.

Orlando   Austin   New York
San Diego   Toronto   London

Requests for permission to make copies of any part of the work
should be mailed to the following address: Permissions Department,
Harcourt, Inc., 6277 Sea Harbor Drive, Orlando, Florida 32887-6777.

www.HarcourtBooks.com

Library of Congress Cataloging-in-Publication Data
Mackall, Dandi Daley.
Eva underground/Dandi Daley Mackall.
p.   cm.
Summary: In 1978, a high school senior is forced by her widowed
father to move from their comfortable Chicago suburb to help with
an underground education movement in communist Poland.
1. Poland—History—1945–1980—Juvenile fiction. [1. Poland—History—
1945–1980—Fiction.   2. Fathers and daughters—Fiction.   3. Grief—Fiction.
4. Coming of age—Fiction.   5. Communist countries—Fiction.]   I. Title.
PZ7.M1905Ev   2006
[Fic]—dc22   2005004195
ISBN-13: 978-0-15-205462-5   ISBN-10: 0-15-205462-6

Text set in Fournier
Designed by Kaelin Chappell Broaddus

First edition

A C E G H F D B

Printed in the United States of America

This is a work of fiction. All the names, characters, places, organizations,
and events portrayed in this book are products of the author's imagination
or are used fictitiously to lend a sense of realism to the story.

To Gosia Muchowiecka Stiff—
Thank you for your courage,
your friendship,
and your faith

Acknowledgments

So many thanks to Tamson Weston, my amazing editor, who believed in me and in this book, and helped me bring this story to life.

EVA
UNDERGROUND

→ 1 ←

Eva Lott popped her seat belt and strained to see past the line of cars stretched in front of her. The stench of exhaust fumes added to her growing nausea. She and her father had driven in sunshine through eastern Austria until they hit this gravel road a hundred yards from the Czech border crossing. Now gray bottom-heavy clouds pressed down on them as if sky and earth conspired to hold the pitiful row of cars in a vise.

"Better fasten your safety belt, Eva," her dad said, his fists white-knuckled at ten and two o'clock on the steering wheel. Sweat beaded on his forehead in spite of the raw cold inside the tiny Renault.

Eva pulled her long black hair into a ponytail and buckled her seat belt. But she didn't feel safer. She tried to tell herself that nothing could really happen to them. It was 1978, and they were Americans. But visions of Communist prison camps and cold Siberian winters crowded her thoughts.

She wanted the line of cars to move, to get on with it. But every time they jerked forward a slot or two, some black car, the windows tinted and secret, pulled up and cut in front. Eva hated her ridiculous urge to hurry the line, especially since the last place she wanted to be was where she was going—the other side of that border, Communist Eastern Europe. It was the same urge she'd felt almost two years ago, when the stalled line had been heading to the Chicago cemetery to bury her mother. Eva had tried not to stare at the hearse in front of them, with its cream-colored pleated curtains drawn over tinted windows. Her mom hated curtains. "Curtains ruin sunlight, Eva," she'd said more than once. "They make us miss what's going on in our own neighborhoods."

The Renault jerked forward. Eva tried to crank her window open, but it wouldn't budge.

"Are you all right, Eva?" her dad asked, his gaze darting to the rows of barbed wire running alongside the gravel road.

"Uh-huh." What could she say?

Of course she wasn't all right. Instead of starting her senior year in Chicago with her boyfriend, Matt, she was headed toward the Iron Curtain. She'd half expected an actual curtain made of iron. But the barbed wire, separating the free world from Communism, seemed even more threatening.

She sat back and rubbed her arms to get the circulation

going. Beyond the barbed wire, a small field ended in more barbed wire. The clouds slipped apart, and light tried to break through the bank of dismal gray. In that second, Eva glimpsed tall wooden towers, spaced a few yards apart like telephone poles. In each tower stood uniformed guards.

Eva squinted, trying to make out the face of the nearest Communist soldier. She wanted him to look familiar, like people she'd known in Chicago.

Light glinted off something in the guard's hand.

"Dad!" Eva shouted, the realization sinking in. "He's got a machine gun!" She wheeled in the seat to check behind them. "Let's go back. It's not too late!"

"Take it easy, Eva," Dad said, his clipped words telling her that *he* wasn't. "It's okay. The guards aren't concerned about us. They're more worried about their own people escaping to freedom."

In a minute, he'd be giving her statistics on border crossings, names and dates of escapes, the entire history of the Soviet occupation of Poland and Czechoslovakia.

"Just act normal," he instructed.

They were only seven or eight cars away from the border now. The gravel road had deteriorated into a frozen mud path.

Ahead, Eva could see the guardhouse, a shack with a window in front and sawhorse barriers all around it. One car at a time was motioned up to the gate's arm. Machine-gun–toting soldiers strutted everywhere—at the gate, down the row, leaning into car windows.

A battered gray car was pulled out of line and directed to the curb beside the guardhouse. Eva watched as three guards in steel-gray uniforms and tall brown boots surrounded the car. Two of the soldiers lifted their weapons and aimed at the driver as he got out. The third soldier, the only one with a furry hat instead of a little military lid, shouted something at the man.

"What are they going to do?" Eva asked. She expected them to shoot, the sound to explode at any moment.

Dad didn't answer. The line of cars didn't advance.

The furry-hat soldier used the butt of his gun to shove the driver toward the guardhouse. The man stumbled. One of the soldiers laughed, then took the man's arm and dragged him inside.

"He's Czech, not American," Eva's dad muttered.

Eva could see into the guardhouse through the filthy glass window. The man's head bobbed between soldiers. She heard a cry. Then the man doubled over and disappeared. More cries pierced the cold air. Then they stopped.

The line inched forward.

"Dad—," Eva cried.

"It'll be all right," he said, cutting her off.

Eva glanced through the back window at the cars lined up behind them, hemming them in. She tried to convince herself that her dad was right. The Czech man was all right. And the soldiers wouldn't mess with American citizens. After all, they hadn't done anything, hadn't even made it into Poland yet.

But she couldn't stop trembling.

The inspection went on for the next thirty minutes, one car at a time. It wasn't like they searched the cars or the passengers. A guard asked each driver questions, took passports and visas, disappeared inside the guardhouse, then came back out, returned the papers, and motioned the car on. Dad turned off the engine between moves to conserve fuel, which had cost close to three dollars a gallon at the last stop in Austria.

Eva needed to stretch her legs, but nobody had gotten out of a car since the poor Czech man had. His car still stood crooked against the curb, where he'd left it.

Three cars and it would be their turn. A short guard, his machine gun slung over one shoulder, frowned down the row of vehicles. His gaze seemed to take in the whole line, which was longer than when Eva and her dad had joined it. His head moved slowly, as if he were examining each car with his X-ray vision. When he got to the Renault, his head froze. Even from where she sat, Eva could see the man's scarred cheek, his eyes slits in leather. She willed him to go on, to look at the next car and the next. But he didn't.

"He's coming to us!" she cried, clutching her dad's elbow.

The soldier raised his machine gun and marched straight to their car. He tapped on the driver's window with the tip of his gun and nodded for her dad to roll down the window.

Eva felt dizzy, like she might puke.

Her dad fumbled with the window, but then got it down halfway. "Hello, sir."

"The passports," Eva whispered.

Dad, who was the most organized person Eva knew, felt in three pockets before coming up with the papers and handing them out the window.

The guard slung his gun back across his shoulder and took their passports. Page by page, he examined each document, studying their faces when he got to the photos. *"Účel vaší cesty?"*

"Uh-h-huh," Dad stammered.

Eva knew he hadn't understood. She and her dad had taken the same crash Polish Berlitz course, but Dad hadn't caught on. He could quote *Paradise Lost* or *Hamlet* without missing a word. He could conjugate Polish verbs and ace written vocab tests. But after weeks of intensive language classes, all he could say in Polish was "I am a tourist. I eat my peas on a knife."

Eva was the opposite. She'd picked up Polish without studying. She couldn't have spelled a single word right, but she was a born mimic, and languages stuck. She'd barely made it through chemistry and algebra, but she'd aced three years of French without cracking a book.

Eva leaned in front of her dad. *"Przepraszam. Mówimy po angielsku."* Sorry. We speak English. Their Berlitz instructor had told them that Czechs understood Polish, and Poles understood Czechoslovakian.

The guard's lips tightened. He repeated his demand—in Czechoslovakian: *"Účel vaší cesty?"*

Eva understood enough. "He asked why we're visiting."

Her dad smiled at the soldier. *"Turysta!"* It was the word for *tourist*, but Eva wasn't sure Scarface had understood.

The guard did an about-face and jogged back to the guardhouse. Eva could see him talking to two other guards, the three of them hurling dagger glances at the *Amerykanie*.

Dad stared straight ahead and started the engine. Gas fumes sneaked into the car, mixing with the old metallic smells.

Scarface burst out of the guardhouse with three guards on his tail. The man's gaze locked onto Eva. She couldn't look away. She watched as he pulled a whistle from around his neck, lifted it to his mouth, and without blinking, blew.

The shrill cry of the whistle traveled through her blood, as four Czechoslovakian border guards ran toward them, their machine guns raised and aimed.

➠ 2 ⬻

Tomek Muchowiecki shuffled in the long line of students waiting to register with the Łódź authorities at the Uniwersytet Łódzki. Every Pole had to be signed in to a city or village so the government would know where its people were every minute of their lives. Here, he would record a residence and get a schedule of classes. He'd stood behind a chain-smoker for nearly two hours in the smoke-filled stone auditorium, where gray light poked through smudges in the window high above the vaulted ceiling.

For the hundredth time, he leaned around to see what the problem was. The heavyset woman behind the table was leaning over, talking to the other fat woman, who should have been servicing the line next to his.

"Bardzo przepraszam."

Tomek heard the apology before he felt the bump. He

turned in time to see the bright red hair of Grażyna Piłsudska. She had gone to school with Tomek's brother, Tadeusz. Tomek felt the note she'd shoved in his hand, but he knew better than to even glance at it as she retreated, her head down.

Watching her walk away, Tomek could picture Tadeusz by her side. It was strange the way children who died got frozen in age. To eleven-year-old Tomek, Tadeusz, seven years his elder, had seemed like a man when the Polish militia gunned him down in the Gdańsk riots of 1970. Yet now, at nineteen, Tomek was the elder.

The line advanced, with one student walking away, eyes down.

The note made Tomek's palm sweat. He glanced behind him, pretending to check the line's length. Was anyone watching him? Had anyone seen Grażyna pass him the note? She shouldn't have done it, no matter what she had to tell him—not here, where gray-suited militia leaned against walls. Russian KGB, secret service, had a direct hand in training the Polish military, and the Soviets hated intellectuals.

On one side of the line, near the front, a young militia held his rifle at the ready and tried to look severe. Across from him, on the other side of the line, an older officer, the white, spread-winged eagle on his collar, eyed would-be students and scribbled his observations on a clipboard. Of the two, Tomek feared the man with the clipboard more. Some things were worse than death. If your name showed up on certain lists, you were denied entry to the university, to higher professions, to a life worth living in Poland.

The line shuffled backward to make room for a well-fed man, his single strand of black hair plastered across his head. He wore a suit that could not have been purchased in Poland, not even with American dollars or deutsche marks. The man, accompanied by a boy, most likely his son, dressed in real blue jeans, stepped up to the table and gave the woman his name.

The fat woman behind the table sat up straight and smiled, her thin lips disappearing around wide, yellow teeth. *"Proszę pana?"*

Tomek should have been used to such injustice by now, but his skin crawled at the boy's smug expression. Communist party members reaped daily privileges, but no one complained at line jumping or the free services they demanded. Poles knew better.

This man's son might have had failing grades, but he'd find a choice place reserved for him at the university, and all his expenses would be paid. Tomek, on the other hand, had studied longer hours than any of his companions, knowing he would need the highest marks to gain entry. He had slept on the floor of his uncle's flat in order to work in Łódź all summer to save for university books.

The ridiculous woman straightened her hair and grinned up at the party leader, instantly handing over papers to sign.

While all eyes were on the well-dressed man, Tomek unfurled the note in his hand and risked a glance. It read: *Your laundry is ready at 9:45.*

So Grażyna was also part of Father Blachnicki's plan. The message meant that the bus to Kraków was scheduled to leave at 9:45, in fifteen minutes. That could not be helped. If the bus departed on time, a rarity in Poland, then Tomek would not be on it. He would not leave without a university schedule of classes. Registering at a university was merely a cover—for the others. Not so for Tomek. He would study poetry. He would pass his exams. Father B.'s plan was to use the American Professor Lott to train writers underground. His spiritual movement, Oasis, had printed banned New Testaments in Polish, giving Father B. control of an illegal printing press. Tomek had no intention of getting involved in the politics of Father B. He would go there and earn money as an interpreter, money he would use for university studies. And that was all.

Tomek glanced at the broken face of the wall clock: 9:41. The bus may have been pulling out of the station at that moment. He might yet run and catch it. As a young boy in Brzegi, Tomek had settled difficult decisions by asking himself, "What would my brother do?" If he asked this question now, the answer would have been simple: *Do the most important thing for Poland and for God.* Tadeusz would have left this line and run after the bus.

But Tomek had not asked himself that question for a long time, and he would not ask it now. Another bus might not come along until nightfall. But this was not his problem. Unsmiling, the party leader and his son walked away, the boy's school schedule stuffed into the back pocket of his Levi's.

Tomek looked away, avoiding their gaze. It was best to be invisible.

Tomek sensed he was being watched, although he couldn't find the eyes. Again he cursed Grażyna for passing him the note that still burned in his pocket. Then he cursed himself for having a bad thought toward someone his brother had cared for.

There remained only the smoker in front of him. "But I must be on this list!" the fellow insisted. "I have my receipt here!" He took out a paper and showed it to the fat woman.

The woman sighed and waved her hand at him, as if shooing away a fly. "Next!"

"But I am sure—" He sounded close to tears.

The woman snapped her fingers and looked to the militia.

"I am sorry," said the smoker. "No problem." He hurried away, leaving Tomek at the head of the line.

"Tomek Muchowiecki," he said, handing her his paper.

She didn't take it. Instead, without a word, she stood up and waddled behind a curtain. Minutes passed. Tomek stole glances at the militia. More time passed. Maybe he should have left the line, taken the bus as Grażyna instructed. Maybe the note had been a warning.

He'd almost made up his mind to bolt from the line and run for the bus station, when the fat woman returned.

She sniffed and wiped crumbs from her mouth with the back of her pudgy hand. A red glob of *pączki* jelly hung from the woman's upper lip, highlighting the dark hairs that grew there. She took his receipt, stuffed it into an envelope, pulled a piece of paper from a box, and handed the paper to him.

Tomek signed the paper and was handed a schedule of classes: sociology, Russian, mathematics, science. Not the courses he had asked for. But it was a start. He would study for the final exams, return to take them, and he would pass. He folded the schedule and placed it in his pocket, covering the note from Grażyna.

Tomek trotted across ulica Narutowicza. He was over an hour late but knew the bus might well have been as late as he. He couldn't shake the sense of being watched, even now as he cut through industrial back lots, across idle railway tracks, to the bus station.

Black fumes floated above the grayed stone blocks, or apartment buildings. They looked alike, pale and shapeless lumps, ugly as Stalin's backside. But the waiting list for a one-room block apartment was seven to fifteen years. His uncle and aunt had been divorced for four years; yet they still shared their apartment for want of another.

Tomek jogged through the small bus station, not stopping to buy a ticket. A dozen Poles waited outside, half of them smoking. No one ever seemed in a hurry except him.

Only one bus sat against the curb, the motor running. The number twelve. Tomek's bus to Kraków. Tadeusz would have called it a "God appointment," but Tomek had not seen things that way for quite a while.

He stepped onto the crowded bus and passed his money to the front. As he did every time he entered a new place, he scanned the crowd, trying to memorize faces so he would recognize a *watcher*.

The door swished shut, and the bus lurched forward. The stench of oil mixed with smells passengers brought on with them—onion, leeks, and vodka. A young boy got up and gave his seat to an old woman. As many women stood in the aisles as men.

"Tomek! *Tutaj!*" It was Grażyna calling him. So she was not just a courier; she was joining the group in Zakopane. She would be older than the others. Perhaps Father B. had enlisted her for special duties.

Tomek edged sideways through the standing passengers to the middle of the bus, where Grażyna sat with a tall straight-haired boy, who looked slightly older than Tomek, but not so old as Grażyna.

"Janek," Grażyna whispered, "this is Tomek."

Janek nodded.

"Tomek Muchowiecki," she added.

The boy scooted up straight and offered his hand to Tomek. "You are Tadeusz's brother!"

He was talking too loud. Two heads turned their way. One, a woman in a tattered gold scarf, looked familiar.

Tomek shook Janek's hand, wishing they had taken different buses. At least he would get off at Kraków, and they could find another bus heading south to Zakopane.

"Your brother is a hero!" Janek didn't seem to notice or care about the heads turning their way. "Tadeusz Muchowiecki is known to the KOR and Young Poland alike."

"*Janek, shush,*" Grażyna whispered. But it was too late. People in many rows could have heard Janek. The woman in the gold scarf turned and glared.

Janek let out a harsh laugh. "You are both scared rabbits!"

Tomek had known others like Janek, men who had to thumb their noses at the government the way childish men mocked a bully to his face. They blew up statues of Lenin, dealt openly in black-market trade, reveled in stirring up trouble in the streets.

The bus stopped every block on the way out of the city. They were more than an hour late already and would be much later than that by the time the bus finally pulled into Kraków.

So the American professor will just have to wait, Tomek thought. *Welcome to Poland.*

⇥ 3 ⇤

Eva watched the border guards close in on them. "Dad! Do something!" she cried, gripping the dashboard with both hands.

"Sit tight," he whispered.

Scarface and another guard jogged to the rear of the car. Eva felt a jolt as the guard stepped on their back bumper. Two more soldiers took the front, one at each of their windows.

The furry-hat Czech guard, the only one without a machine gun, strolled up to her dad's window. He said something Eva couldn't understand, his words coming through a bushy mustache, dingy from cigarette smoke.

Her father, still trying to smile, held both palms up, the international sign for *Don't shoot*.

Furry Hat reached in and turned off the ignition.

Then he stepped back. "Out!" At least that's what Eva thought he said.

She was sure of it when one of the guards yanked open her door. A rush of cold air slapped her cheek.

Eva climbed out, not bothering to grab her purse. Outside it felt eerily silent, as quiet as inside the car. The line of cars had stopped. Drivers and passengers kept their heads down.

Eva's dad hurried around to her and took her hand. She couldn't remember the last time they'd held hands.

"Can I help you . . . find anything?" Dad asked, his deep voice trailing off.

They ignored him. Furry Hat took the key from the ignition and tossed it to a guard, who opened the trunk. Eva and her dad had only been able to bring two suitcases each—two, for a whole year. Eva thought she'd deserved a medal for leaving so much behind. And now she had to watch as both of her suitcases were flung into the road. Her dad's suitcases were yanked from the backseat and ransacked.

Scarface snapped open Eva's plaid bag, the one that had been her mother's, and rifled through it. He touched her pajamas, her underwear, the Peter Frampton T-shirt Matt had given her the night before she left. The guard opened her journal, showed it to the taller guard, and threw it back in—a fish too little to keep.

Eva kept her eye on the furry-hat soldier, who seemed to be in charge. He leaned into the backseat, lifted her jacket, the map. Then he stopped. He barked something to the others, and they stopped searching suitcases. She had the sensation of watching a train wreck in slow motion.

A stillness closed around the furry-hat guard, a coiled threat as he backed slowly out of the car, holding a book in one hand.

Eva tried to remember if she'd left her book there. What had she read on the plane to Vienna? But she'd carried all paperbacks so she could fit more in. It had to be her dad's. With a bitter aftertaste rising up her throat, she realized what the book was—her mother's Bible.

"You brought a Bible?" she whispered through clenched teeth, not daring to face her dad. How could he have been so careless? Even Eva had heard about "Bible smugglers," people who sneaked in Bibles to Communist countries, where Bibles were outlawed. "In plain sight?"

Dad whispered out of the side of his mouth, staring straight ahead. "They told me I could bring a personal Bible. They said not to hide it or the guards would get suspicious."

"*Precz z nim!*" shouted the short soldier. He swung his gun, making it clear he wanted them to step away from the car. He blew his whistle. Three more guards came running.

Eva and her dad huddled closer together, shivering without their coats, unsheltered from the harsh wind. As they watched, seven soldiers rooted through every inch of the Renault. The men poked around under the hood, crawled underneath the car, took out the entire backseat and threw it on the ground.

When nothing was left, no possible hiding place, the officers shouted at them, pointing their rifles at the mess they'd made. All but Scarface returned to the guardhouse. Conscious of his unrelenting stare, Eva grabbed their things and shoved them into suitcases, while Dad struggled to put the seats back into the car.

Cars chugged around them, making them a blip in the straight line of vehicles inching to the gate. Eva glanced in as the cars passed. Only one person dared to look at them, a girl much younger than Eva, her head covered with a white shawl or scarf. The Czech girl turned sad, green eyes to Eva and nodded, as if apologizing for the entire Czechoslovakian military.

Eva nodded back, watching until the girl was a blur on a gray horizon.

"Let's go, Eva!" Dad called.

They climbed in, and Eva saw her father's hand shake as he stuck the key into the ignition. The starter churned, three times, and she felt her stomach lurch with every try. Finally the engine sputtered and caught. The car behind them stopped, and Dad eased back into the line heading toward the gate.

But Scarface ran out at them, shaking his gun. He motioned for the car behind them to go ahead. Then he pointed his gun to the end of the line.

Her dad had to drive one wheel in the ditch to retrace the long row of cars and fall in at the end of the line.

Three hours later they crossed the border into Czechoslovakia.

Eva squeezed her eyes shut. She wanted to go to sleep

and wake up back home in Chicago, sitting between Matt and Melanie in the noisy high school cafeteria.

Two months ago, Eva had been biking home from the Y, her long wet hair blowing in black tangles across her face. She couldn't wait to tell her dad that she'd made the varsity swim team. There hadn't been much good Eva-news lately. Maybe this would make up for some of the bad.

She'd eased her bike past the Buick in the garage and taken the steps to the kitchen. "I'm home!"

Eva heard footsteps upstairs. That was weird. She'd figured her dad would be snitching leftovers by now. They'd stopped waiting on each other for meals. Trying to keep up the conversation had been too hard on both of them. "Dad? You up there?"

"Coming!" Her father's voice had a natural pitch half an octave lower than everyone else's. Eva's mom used to say that was why she'd married him.

Eva started up the stairs and met her dad coming down.

"Dad, guess what! I—" But the look on his face made her stop. His eyebrows twitched, the way they had the night he'd told her about Mom, about the cancer.

"What is it?" Her ears pounded. "Are you sick?"

"What? Oh . . . no, Eva. No." He sat on the step and awkwardly dangled his long arms over his knees. "I'm fine."

She could feel the breath go out of her. A picture flashed through Eva's mind—her mother, curled up in a hospital bed, her breath no longer strong enough to move the white folds of the cotton sheet.

"Sorry I frightened you," Dad said. "Nothing's

wrong. In fact, everything is fine . . . great, really. Well, it might not seem so great to you at first. But once you get used to the idea . . ."

Eva knew her father had as much trouble talking to her as she did to him. "Come in the kitchen and tell me what's up. I'll pop popcorn." It was one of the few things they had left in common, a passion for buttered popcorn. Eva's mom had been their path to each other. She'd forged tiny trails to keep their lives intersecting—meals, vacations, conversation starters. When she died, the path got overgrown. Neither of them seemed to have the vision to see the old path or the energy to plow a new one.

Eva headed for the kitchen.

Dad didn't budge. His six-and-a-half-foot frame shadowed half the staircase. She waited. Now that she knew he didn't have cancer, she wanted him to say what he had to say, so she could tell him *her* news.

"I didn't want to say anything until I was sure. You've been so touchy lately . . . I thought . . . Well, remember that Polish priest, the one who came to the university? Father Blachnicki?"

Eva shrugged.

Her dad kept talking—about the priest's underground movement, Oasis, and the TKN, a group of teachers and radicals. "They're the only ones printing the truth in that country—the hope of Poland, Eva."

He'd probably told her all this before. Maybe once she would have actually listened, cared. Not now. Now she knew better. Her mother's death had taught her that much. The only thing worth listening to was here and now.

Her dad squeezed the bridge of his nose. "They need university teachers to help."

Eva stared at him, unable to move.

"I'm in line for a sabbatical. Father Blachnicki heard I was almost a priest once—all but the vows. And I worked newspapers for a while. Long story short, it's a chance to do something that really matters. Poland, Eva! Your great-grandmother came from Łódź."

Eva studied her father. She could almost see herself in his big dark eyes—the eyes half the women in church claimed she and her dad shared: *Eva, you have your father's eyes.*

He had to be kidding. "Yeah, right, Dad. Poland." Even Dad wasn't that crazy. She walked to the kitchen, got out a fresh bag of popcorn, and plugged in the popper.

Dad stood slump-shouldered in the doorway. "Eva, we have to talk."

His voice, empty of the slightest hint of teasing, caught her off guard. Her stomach tightened. Refusing to look at him, she opened the plastic bag and watched the hard gold kernels of popcorn ping, then cascade into the popper, past the fill line, to the top.

"It's just for a year," Dad said. "You can finish high school through correspondence and still make Northwestern next fall." His voice sounded as if it were underwater, thick and distant. "Even *you* have to admit you've been getting in nothing but trouble around here, Eva. It will do us both good to get away—from this house, from all the memories."

She watched the kernels overflow onto the counter, bouncing to the kitchen tiles her mother had laid with her own hands. How could he even think about leaving this house?

". . . tough lately . . . fresh chance . . . write letters . . ." Dad kept talking, saying things that didn't make sense.

Eva had clutched the empty plastic popcorn bag in her fist and walked straight past him, down the hall, and out the door. Then she was running, faster and faster in the dark, under a fingernail moon and a handful of stars, past houses that glowed with TV light and shadows of normal families.

"Eva?" Her dad cleared his throat and said it louder. "Eva?"

"I'm awake." She sat up and looked through the windshield, but the only thing visible was a patch of road directly in front of the Renault's headlights.

"I've been wondering," Dad said as they bumped over a rut in the frozen mud. "What did that Czech guard at the gate say when he gave us back our papers? Did you catch any of it?"

Eva bit her cheek. She almost wished she hadn't understood the man's last words to them. "He said . . . he said we only have a twenty-four-hour transit visa. And if we're not out of Czechoslovakia in twenty-four hours, we'll spend the rest of our lives here."

⇥ 4 ⇤

"Excuse me," Tomek said, his anger at Janek outweighing his fear. "I will stand at the back of the bus." He nodded to Grażyna and moved away before Janek could say anything else to get them into trouble.

It was misting when the bus bounced over the cobbled streets into Kraków. Tomek hurried off before Janek and Grażyna could question him. He had no desire to tell Janek that Professor Lott was waiting at Wawel and had likely been there for hours.

Tomek's stomach rumbled as he crossed through Main Market Square to the southern tip of Old Town. It was his favorite part of Kraków. He had eaten the bread and apple from his pack, his only luggage. Traveling light aroused less suspicion. Later, he could get supplies and clothes from his father's home in Brzegi, an hour's journey from Zakopane.

The city fell silent as dusk blanketed the streets and turned alleys into shadowy mazes. Tomek headed up Wawel Hill, past the horse statue of his brother's namesake, Tadeusz Kościuszko, who had fought in the American Revolution and the Polish fight for independence.

He circled the cathedral, glad that Polish Septembers kept most tourists away. Father B. had given instructions to meet the American professor at the entrance to the Dragon's Cave.

Many things could have happened to the American professor. He might have changed his mind. Poland, after all, was not his country. Why should he take this risk? Or he might not have been granted entry to the East. The only visas given to Americans were three-month tourist visas, and those were not easy to secure. Worse, his car might have broken down in Czechoslovakia.

Father B. had offered no description of Dr. Lott, no help in identifying him. But few Americans ventured behind the Iron Curtain. And if they did, they stuck with guided tours in Warsaw. The lone American would stand out like Adidas in a Polish shoe shop.

From the vista at the cave entrance, Tomek looked down with pride at the castle of Polish kings, now inhabited by Father B.'s friend, Cardinal Karol Wojtyła, Archbishop of Kraków. Men and women in orange uniforms swept the street beside the castle. A few Poles ambled down the hill.

Then he saw two Americans headed toward him. The

man's great size and blue stocking cap marked him as American. Tomek might have taken him for Professor Lott, if it were not for the girl with him. As they climbed the hill, the slender girl, probably in her late teens, was walking backward, shouting into the man's face. She had thick black amazing hair, ridged like plowed fields. Even in her heavy coat and tiny beret, she was beautiful, perhaps an American model. Tomek tried not to stare at them.

As they got closer, he could make out the girl's angry English words: "We can't keep walking around here for the rest of our lives! They're not coming. Please, can't we just take a taxi to the airport and go back home?"

Tomek smiled to himself. He had known several attractive Polish girls at school, and they were all as ill-tempered as this one.

He stopped smiling. The man was looking his way. Tomek shifted his weight from one foot to the other and pretended to study the view of the castle. He willed himself invisible.

The man was jogging toward him, waving one arm.

The last thing Tomek needed was to draw attention to himself.

"Um . . . say there?" The man stood a head taller than Tomek, who had always been the tallest in his class. "Are you waiting for someone?"

Tomek pretended he didn't understand.

"Amerykanski!" The man pointed to himself. "American professor? . . . Um . . . Father B.?"

Tomek winced. "Professor Lott?"

"Yes! We made it!" He turned to the girl. "Eva! We've

found them!" Turning back to Tomek, he said, "I'd like you to meet my daughter, Eva Lott. Eva, this is . . . I'm sorry. I didn't catch your name."

"Tomek."

She nodded, her lips pressed into a thin white line.

Tomek wondered if Father B. would be as surprised as he was that the professor had brought along his daughter. He surveyed the grounds to see if they were being watched. "We must go. It is a long drive to Zakopane. You have a car, yes?" He was aware that his English did not sound like theirs. He had learned fluent English from a London priest, a friend of his father's.

"We bought a used car in Vienna," Professor Lott explained. "They wouldn't let us drive up here, so we left the car parked in front of our hotel. I hope that's all right. Hotel Europejski. Do you know it?"

Tomek knew it. It was the best hotel in the region, where all Americans stayed. "Room eleven?"

"That's right!" Professor Lott looked astonished. "How did you know that?"

"It is where they put all foreigners," Tomek explained. "I hope you did not talk much. They . . ." He couldn't think of the right slang word. "They are tapping wires?"

"Wiretap? They bug the room?" The professor turned to his daughter. "We didn't say anything, did we, Eva?"

"We said it was a dump," she muttered.

"I sure hope we didn't say anything about why we're here."

So did Tomek. Father B. should have warned them about security. Maybe he hadn't wanted to scare them off.

The girl didn't say anything else, but her father would not stop. All the walk down Wawel Hill he recounted their crossing experiences with the border militia. They had gotten lost and skidded into a ditch near Bruno. "All I could think about," the professor continued too loudly, "was what that Czech guard had said about getting out in twenty-four hours no matter what."

"It is true advice." Tomek hated the sound of his English, which was much better when he wasn't so nervous. He wished he could return to Łódź, start his studies now, instead of babysitting the Americans.

Professor Lott sighed. "But the ol' Renault started first try and kept going all the way to the Polish border. Had a bit of a scare when the Polish guard found my Bible. Father B. told me not to hide it. But since that hadn't worked well at the Czech border, this time I hid the Bible under Eva's seat."

"Which was the first place the border guard looked," Eva added. Tomek watched her breath come out in frost clouds.

"True . . ." Professor Lott seemed anxious to continue. Tomek wanted to ask him to wait until they were safely in the car, but he could not be rude. "But the *Polish* guard just looked through my Bible, then handed it back gently, as if it were glass."

"Not many of our people own the Old Testament of the Bible, though most have the New Testament in Polish now."

"I wish I could have given him mine." The professor stopped in front of the hotel and all but pointed at his car. "Well, here we are!"

"We should begin our journey," Tomek suggested. "The drive is three hours in the daylight." He opened the passenger door to climb into the backseat, but he couldn't get in. Two of the largest suitcases he had ever seen took up the entire backseat. "May I put these in the trunk, please?"

Professor Lott lifted his wool hat and scratched his head. "I'm afraid the trunk is full with *my* bags. Sorry. Just push them on the floor."

As Tomek squeezed into the seat, ending up with a gigantic plaid suitcase on his lap, he marveled that this spoiled American girl could have enough possessions to fill such bags. She would never survive in Poland. He would give her two days tops.

⤞ 5 ⤝

Eva took her seat at the long table, wedging herself onto the wooden bench, between her dad and Krystyna. Tomek sat across from her, glaring disapproval, but it wasn't her fault she was late. It really wasn't. She'd been last in line for the bathroom. She'd refused to go ahead of Krystyna and Grażyna, even when they'd insisted.

Tomek Muchowieski was six feet tall, lean but solid, with thick black hair that was curlier than Eva's dad's, and brown eyes that didn't seem to miss anything. Eva thought he acted like he was ninety-one instead of nineteen.

She closed her eyes for the blessing and prayed that when she opened them, she'd be anywhere but Pani Kurczak's freezing basement in Zakopane, Poland.

"Ava, eat?" Krystyna asked, pushing her wild blond hair from her forehead.

Eva, she wanted to scream. Not *Ava.* It was a little thing, and she tried not to let it get to her. After all, she could barely pronounce the names of most of the people sitting at that table. They sounded more like sneezes than names. Still, every time they called her *Ava,* it made her feel farther away from home, as if she weren't even the same person as when she left.

Eva was starving. For the five days she and her father had been in Poland, she hadn't seen meat or ice cream or even popcorn. The few stores in Zakopane were a joke. Shelves in the butcher shop were totally empty, except for rows of tins without labels, stacked behind the barren meat counter.

She and her dad had stayed up late again, arguing in whispers so they wouldn't be heard through the paper-thin walls of their room. "I could live with Melanie," she'd reasoned, "just until I finish my senior year. Then if you're still here, I'll come back. I could spend the summer here." But she'd known, even as she'd argued, that her dad would never let her go back to Chicago without him.

"I know you don't see it now, Eva," her dad had whispered back. "But one day you'll be proud to say you played a part in Polish independence, that you knew Father Blachnicki—"

"We're barely Polish!" she'd interrupted. "And you're not even Catholic anymore."

"I changed denominations so your mother and I could go to the same church," he'd countered. "But it's the same

God, Eva. And I'd want to be part of the struggle in Poland, even if I were zero percent Polish."

Her dad hadn't budged. Nobody won arguments with Professor Lott. And so here she was, trapped in this place with no friends, no phone, no TV, and nothing to eat.

On the plastic green-plaid tablecloth sat one large plate with breakfast: bread . . . with something on it. Of course. Every breakfast was the same. Bread with something on it. Suppers, too. And she hadn't complained. She'd thanked them, knowing this was all they had. But it didn't keep her stomach from wishing for something more.

Krystyna reached for the plate, then held it out to Eva.

Eva's dad leaned down and whispered, "Take one. Don't be rude."

If she had a nickel for every time Dad had said that, *Don't be rude,* she could have bought an airplane ticket to freedom.

Eva swallowed hard and eyed the cracked yellow plate stacked high with a pyramid of brownish bread that smelled like a cellar. On one side of the plate was bread with the fishy paste stuff she'd come to distrust. On the other side, bread with rust-colored jelly.

But one piece looked different. The center slice of bread looked like it was topped with a thick chunk of white cheese. *Cheese!* Eva was so hungry, the thought of something as familiar as cheese made her taste buds ache.

But would it be rude to take it? There was only one thick white chunk on bread. Eva glanced around the table at the ten faces watching. They grinned at her.

Even Tomek pointed to the top piece of bread and nodded for her to go ahead and take it.

"Ava, eat," Krystyna urged, pointing to the choice piece of bread on top.

Only one, but they wanted her to have it. It was what they wanted, right? Her stomach growled. Before her dad could stop her, Eva reached out and grabbed the top piece of bread.

"Eva—," Dad said.

But it was too late. Eva stuffed the bread into her mouth and bit off a big hunk. Her teeth sank too easily through the white chunk. It squished in her mouth and smelled like garbage.

Eva gagged. This wasn't cheese. She glanced up at her dad, her eyes watering, something thick and mushy sticking to her throat.

Her father looked as if he had eaten something sour. "It's lard," he whispered. "Fat is a delicacy over here."

"They have saved it for a long time, a special occasion," Tomek explained.

She had just eaten a mouthful of lard? Fat? Pure fat? It was all she could do not to puke right there.

Eva stared at the plaid tablecloth in front of her until it blurred. *Lard?* She shoved the table to get up, knocking over her glass.

"Ava?"

"Excuse me," she muttered, the lard a lump in her throat.

"Eva? Don't . . ."

She didn't stay long enough to hear the end of her dad's plea, which was no doubt, "Don't be rude."

Eva hurried up the two flights of winding pie-shaped stairs and ran down the hall. Ten students, plus Tomek, lived in Pani Kurczak's house with Eva and her dad. And one bathroom. Pani K.'s house was named Widokówka. They named everything here, and she couldn't pronounce any of them.

She made it to her room and slammed the door behind her. Every time she looked at these walls, the room seemed smaller. And she had to share it with her father.

When they'd arrived with only two suitcases each, the plan had been to have more of their things shipped over once they got settled. But one look at this room—with two narrow beds and one small wardrobe—and even Eva had realized there was no place to put the stuff they had with them. In the end, they had each kept only one of their suitcases and mailed back the other two. It had been the hardest thing she'd been forced to do since arriving in Poland—until now.

Eva plopped onto her bed. She could still taste lard and feel it congealing in her stomach. The rough blanket made her skin itch, but she pulled it around her, anyway. Their only heat came from a pipe that led from Pani K.'s coal-burning oven in the basement, straight up through the house. Breakfast warmed Tomek's room on the first floor. *Obiad*, the big meal of the day, created enough heat to warm the rooms on the second. But the heat hardly ever made it to Eva's third-floor room.

She reached for the notebook and pencil her dad had out on his bed. She'd have given anything—*anything*—for two minutes with Melanie, or one minute with Matt. Until now, she hadn't been able to force herself to write either of them. It hurt too much. But now she had nothing else.

She pictured Matt—tall, blond, handsome Matt. He was the kind of guy parents loved and kids wanted to be like. He was the first to take a dare, first to try cigarettes, first to get drunk. She'd wanted to go out with him for as long as she could remember, but they'd only gotten together during the end of their junior year.

Dear Matt,

You wouldn't believe what it's like here. I miss you so much! You'll never guess—

The pencil broke. Eva looked around for a pencil sharpener. Of course there wasn't one. They probably hadn't invented pencil sharpeners in Poland yet. Her pens were in the pocket of the other suitcase, the lucky one headed home. This was too much. Now she couldn't even write Matt.

Rolling over on her back, Eva stared at the cracked ceiling and tried to imagine Matthew Linden, the amazing hunk, who had chosen her to be his girlfriend. They never talked about love, but she was pretty sure she did love him. Matt could always make her laugh. Man, how she missed that! She hadn't laughed since America. And she wouldn't laugh until she got back.

Eva felt like kicking herself for not making a run for it at the airport. She'd known it would be bad, but not this bad.

Part of her knew she deserved this exile. Her father had made it clear enough that he wanted to get her away from Chicago "for your own good." They both knew what he meant. In the last year or so, he'd busted her half a dozen times for coming home "drunk"—just a couple of beers with Matt or at a party. Her grades had taken a serious nosedive her junior year, too.

But the last straw, the thing her dad couldn't let go, was the call from the security cop at Quick Mart. "Is your daughter Eva Lott?" the cop asked, holding the phone in one hand and Eva's wrist with the other. "This is security down at Quick Mart on Murray. We need you to come down here, Mr. Lott. Your daughter's been caught shoplifting."

She hadn't been, though. Not that day.

A week before her mother's birthday—she would have been forty-three—Eva had wandered into Quick Mart for a cherry Icee, a drink her mom had called "red gold." As the cup filled from the self-serve fountain, Eva had reached over to a row of snacks and idly straightened the packs of gum. Cinnamons and bubble gums had gotten mixed in with spearmints and with Juicy Fruits. Only they didn't all fit in the rack.

Eva had tried to shove the extra pack of spearmint in with the others, but it wouldn't go. So she'd slipped the green packet into her pocket, paid for the Icee, and walked out.

She could still remember the odd realization that she didn't feel guilty. She'd taken the gum without paying for it, and something about it felt right, fair. The gum weighed in the pocket of her purple nylon jacket all afternoon. Matt had picked her up for his game. She'd kept sticking her hand into her pocket—in the car, in the stands during the ball game, later at Pizza Hut—making sure she hadn't imagined the gum. Each time she touched the sharp edges of the pack, she shivered inside. She had taken it. Nobody knew. She could do it again any time she wanted.

She did it two more times that week, always gum, which she never opened. Then on Mom's birthday, she did it again, slipping a pack of cinnamon gum into her pocket and walking out.

She'd gotten to the end of the block when she remembered the first time she'd taken something from a store. She'd been five years old and had grabbed a Hershey's bar from a grocery store display. Mom had made her walk back in, apologize, and return the candy.

Standing on the corner, the cinnamon gum safely in her pocket, Eva had wanted to drop to the sidewalk and cry. Instead, she'd turned around, walked back into Quick Mart, and put the gum back in the rack.

That's when the bald security cop had grabbed her and demanded her name and phone number. Eva hadn't objected, hadn't tried to convince him or her dad that she'd been doing the opposite of stealing, un-stealing.

Her dad had arrived, looking ten times as scared for

her as she was for herself. She'd gotten off with a warning from the security cop and with a lecture on theft and the state of penal institutions in Chicago from her dad.

But she hadn't gotten off, not really. Her father had exiled both of them to Poland, and these four walls had become her prison.

Someone knocked at the door.

Startled, she jerked, and the bed creaked. "What?" she shouted.

Again, the knock.

Eva got up and opened the door.

Krystyna stood there, a good five inches shorter than Eva, though they were both eighteen. Krystyna's blond hair, thin as an angel's, looked as if she had cut it herself, with her eyes closed. She motioned with her head for Eva to follow her.

Instead Eva asked, "Pencil?" She realized she was shouting, as if sheer volume would make Krystyna understand. Lowering her voice, she repeated, "Do you have a pencil?" She reached to the bed and grabbed the broken pencil.

Krystyna pulled a pen from her apron and handed it to Eva.

"Thanks," Eva muttered.

Krystyna stepped closer to Eva, inches away. "Ava, *tutaj*."

Eva stepped back. She wasn't used to standing so close.

Krystyna didn't seem to notice the withdrawal. She put her hand on Eva's arm and leaned in. "Two moments. Ava, come. Wear coat."

Eva forced herself to nod. If she didn't go peacefully, her dad would probably come and drag her out.

Krystyna left, and Eva dashed a note onto Matt's letter: *Matt, I'll finish this later. Right now I'm being forced to go somewhere cold. I have no idea where. If you don't hear from me, send in the Marines.*

⇥ 6 ⇤

By the time Eva had bundled up in every sweater she had left, she was the last one out of the house. She caught sight of her dad through the mist down the lane. He was walking between Tomek and a tall man she hadn't seen before. Although it was mid-morning, the gray sky blended with wet, gray earth to make it dark as night.

"Dad!" Eva called. She stepped into the lane, right into thick mud that sucked up her tennis shoes. Gooey black oozed over the tops of her sneakers, all the way up her ankles and socks.

Krystyna ran back to the rescue. "Poor Ava," she said, taking Eva's hand and pulling. "You will be late to bless the house."

"Did she say *bless a house?*"

Tomek nodded.

Eva's feet came out, but one shoe didn't. The mud slurped, as if satisfied with the great tennis-shoe meal, then it burped up the leftovers.

Tomek retrieved the shoe and knelt to slip it on Eva's foot. Krystyna offered her shoulder for balance. It seemed like a weird Polish version of "Cinderella."

"Are there any paved streets in Zakopane?" Eva asked, pushing her toes into the mud-filled shoe. "Or sidewalks?" She said it in English so only Tomek understood. She wouldn't have wanted to insult Krystyna, who at least tried to be nice.

"We do not need paved streets," Tomek said, shoving her shoe harder than he had to, then letting her foot drop. "Zakopane is a mountain town. We walk, we take horses, or we take to skis in winter."

Eva squinted into the fog. She hadn't seen a mountain since they'd arrived. For all she knew, the whole country was nothing but a big gray cloud.

"The Tatras surround us," Tomek said, as if he'd read her mind. "When the sun comes back, you will see beautiful mountains."

Eva nodded. But she wasn't about to wait for the sun to come out, even if there were mountains. She wouldn't be here that long, thank you very much. She was going back home the first chance she got, whether her dad liked it or not.

Krystyna kept hold of her hand. Ahead of them, Grażyna, who so far hadn't done anything except scrub floors, held hands with one of the other female students. It made Eva uncomfortable. She gently pulled her fingers loose from Krystyna's hand and tried to catch up to her dad.

"Guess we need boots," Dad said after one look at her mud-caked shoes. He turned to the tall man. "Father B., this is my daughter, Eva. Eva, this is Father Blachnicki."

The ancient man in a black raincoat and broad-brimmed hat smiled down at her and shook her hand. He was nearly as tall as her father, but much older, his face cracked into wrinkles.

"Please continue, Professor," Blachnicki said as they kept walking, forcing Eva to step in behind them.

Tomek moved up beside her. "It is good Father B. and your father can talk and not need me. Father B. speaks seven languages. He is a hero to us. In World War Two, he fought in the Polish resistance against Hitler. He was two years in Auschwitz concentration camp. And when the war ended, he was put in prison by the Russians. There, too, he organized resistance."

"I know," Eva mumbled. Her dad had told her and Melanie all about it the night Mel had stayed over to help them pack. Melanie, who belonged to half a dozen causes—save the seals, end wars, save the forests—had been ready to sign on with Father B. right then and there. If Eva had been a better person, more like her mother, Eva knew she might have been caught up in this struggle, too, in the awe they all felt for Father B. But she wasn't a better person. And all she wanted was to be home with Melanie and Matt.

"How much farther to the house that needs to be blessed?" she asked, wondering what it would feel like to believe in blessings again. She had once, before she'd watched her mother die, but she couldn't remember what it had felt like.

"Not far," Tomek answered.

They passed three houses that looked almost like Pani Kurczak's boardinghouse. They reminded Eva of a jigsaw puzzle, a big piece in brick, then a side of concrete block, another side of wood, and a tin roof.

Tomek caught her staring at them. "The houses are not like in America, yes? Here, people must use what they can get, when they can get it."

"We are here!" Krystyna announced, taking Eva's hand again.

A young couple holding a baby stood in the doorway of the smallest house on the street. Their smiles were so big that Eva could see each parent had a tooth missing. The husband looked a little like Tomek, with bushy black hair, wide eyes, and a lean build.

At the doorway, guests took off their shoes and pulled slippers out of their pockets. Eva's dad took off his shoes and went in stocking feet.

Eva held back until everybody else had filed in. Then she took off her muddy shoes. Her socks were soaked through with mud. She didn't know if it would be ruder to go in with muddy socks or with bare feet. She opted for the socks and tiptoed in, glancing back at her muddy footprints.

From the next room, Eva thought she heard wailing. By the time she got there, the sounds came together, and she knew they were singing. Not on key, and not in unison exactly. But she recognized the tune, "This Is the Day That the Lord Has Made." It was one her mother had sung, one they'd both learned in Bible school. A yearning to hear the English words, her mother's voice, burned in her chest.

They sang another song Eva didn't recognize, and then everybody looked to Father B. for the service to start. Eva felt her heart speed up. How were they going to bless the house? She just hoped it wouldn't be too weird.

Marek, another housemate, a university student from Lublin, stepped to the front and handed Father Blachnicki a large dried brown branch. It looked a little like a stick broom. Blachnicki poured water from a small bottle into a bowl and dipped the branch into it.

Eva made her way to her father's side. "Dad, what's going to happen?"

"I have no idea," her dad whispered back.

Father B. took the branch and raised it above his head. As if by silent signal, every head bowed. Eva's dad bowed his head, and so did Eva, although she kept her eyes wide open.

Father B. prayed something and waved the branch. Then everybody looked up. He touched the four walls with the branch, sprinkling them with water.

It was weird, but more funny weird than scary weird. "Is that it?" she asked Tomek, who had sneaked up beside them.

He shook his head no. "Father B. has christened the living room, where friends may gather in the name of Christ."

There was only one room, but Father B. waved the

branch over the daybed and crib. He prayed something that Eva assumed was a bedroom blessing. She recognized the words for *sleep, God, children, always.* It made her think of Matt, the way he'd listen to a ball game on the car radio long after they'd lost good reception, picking up enough words to make out the action.

They followed Father B. into the kitchen area. There was a prayer for the stove, which really didn't need blessing, Eva thought. It was a hundred times more modern than Pani Kurczak's oven.

They blessed the bathroom. Eva couldn't help it. She let out a tiny, muffled laugh.

Only Tomek turned around. "Don't be afraid of different, Eva," he said.

She glared at him. He had no idea of "different." She'd love to drop him in the middle of a Chicago rush hour. See how he felt about different then.

After Father B. blessed the bathroom, Eva thought that had to be it. But he stopped in the middle of the main room to admire a metal fan sitting on the floor.

Eva recalled another fan.

For as long as Eva could remember, her father had been the teacher. Every Christmas there would be at least one great gift she wasn't allowed to play with until her dad had read all of the instructions and could instruct her in how best to play. He knew how to take the fun out of the zoo by explaining natural habitats of penguins and the digestive processes of the African elephant. He was the reason Eva still didn't have her driver's license. Two driving lessons with her dad, which included the aerodynamics of automobiles and the finer points of vehicle maneuverability, had been enough to convince both of them she was better off walking.

Dad was the teacher, but Eva believed she had learned more from her mother. Eva's mom had shown her how to make a blade of grass whistle, how to turn a used straw cover into a wiggly worm, how to greet horses by blowing into their nostrils . . . and how to sing into fans.

Eva could almost hear her mother's voice, singing, *Row, row, row your boat,* inches from the tiny fan, the way the words came back as if they were being cut in pieces and sewn back together wrong.

Remembering, and watching Father B. solemnly wave his branch over the fan and mutter a fan blessing—it was too much. All her emotions squeezed together and erupted in a loud, spit-spraying laugh. She tried to stop it. She covered her mouth with her hands. But it was no use. It only made her laughter explode. Her eyes watered, and she couldn't see the fan or Father B. or anybody.

When she stopped shaking, she gasped for breath. Every eye in the room was turned to her. And nobody else was laughing. Nobody was smiling.

Eva felt her face burn as they kept staring at her.

She looked to her dad, but he wrinkled his forehead and turned to Tomek. "Tomek, will you please apologize to everyone for my daughter."

Eva had never felt so betrayed in her whole life. She turned and ran. Not remembering where she'd come in, she pushed through the first door she found, through the kitchen, through another door.

Steps led down to a cellar. Eva took them. At the bottom of the stairs, she looked around. The walls were dirt, and splintered rafters spread across the ceiling.

How could her father have brought her to this place? How could he take their side? She would never let him do that to her again.

Eva slid down to the ground, pulled her knees up to her chin, and cried.

When she couldn't cry anymore, she leaned back against the cold wall. That's when she heard a high whining. She stayed still. Maybe it was her imagination. Maybe it was her.

But the whine came again, longer and wilder.

Eva got up and followed the sound to the back of the cellar, to a small wooden door. The whine didn't sound human. She slid the door to the side.

A fuzzy, scraggly, scrawny puppy burst out of a pantry filled with potatoes.

Eva took the dog in her arms. He smelled like rotten potatoes. "You poor thing! Who did this to you? You're okay. You're okay now."

She buried her head in the dirty, reddish fur. "I'll get you out of here," she vowed. "I'll get us both out of here and back to civilization if it's the last thing I do."

Dear Melanie,

Writing you and Matt is the only thing that keeps me from going insane! Still no mail from anybody. We can't get mail here. Somebody is supposed to sneak our letters out to Vienna and bring our letters in to us. It feels like a spy movie. *Like hearing from you guys would threaten Communism?*

It's been a week since the house blessing (and that's something I'd rather not talk about). Sometimes I dream about you and me and Matt and even Mrs. Rowe's English class. Then I wake up, shivering with the cold, and figure out that I'm still in Poland. That's the worst—that second of slipping out of the dream . . . back into the nightmare.

I have only one good thing to report. I got a dog! Samson the Great! Rescued from the basement of the blessed house. Tomek said the people who lived there before the house was blessed probably couldn't take the dog with them to their new home. So they just left him to fend for himself! And I'm the only one here who thinks that was a terrible thing to do.

Don't ask me how or why, but Dad didn't say anything when I brought the dog to our room. (Of course he wasn't talking much to me after the house blessing. Don't ask.) Samson, who is the sweetest ball of fluff you can imagine, growls whenever Dad gets too close, which isn't very often because the growling is mutual.

Pani Kurczak took some convincing. She finally agreed I could keep the piesek, *only if I could wash the potato smell out of him. It took a whole day and five baths, but Samson earned the Pani K. stamp of approval.*

By the way, Pani *means "Mrs." in Polish.* Kurczak *means "chicken," and in a way, Pani K. does look like one. Her nose is so sharp she could use it as a weapon.*

You'd die if you saw my wardrobe. It's freezing here, so I've had to wear everything I own . . . every single day!

Talk about a fashion statement! The only difference in my outfit is what I wear on top. Don't tell Matt! Let him still think of me the way I was . . . if he still thinks of me at all.

Mel, I want you to double-check with your mom to make sure it would be okay if I stayed with you guys the rest of the school year. But you can't let it get back to Dad. Maybe ask it as a hypothetical. If it's not okay, then I'll sleep in your car. But I can't stay here.

Promise not to say anything to anybody, not even Matt. Not until I'm actually there. I'll find a way to get Samson and me out of Poland if it kills me.

See you soon!

Love, Eva

⤙ 7 ⤚

"It's too much," Tomek muttered, shutting the door to his room and rushing down for Professor Lott's class. *I will tell him today that I quit.*

He turned around and nearly tripped over Grażyna, who was rag-polishing the floor. Her red hair caught the morning sunshine that streaked through the windows and up the stairs.

"Tomek, *tłumacz*." She sat back on her heels and grinned at him. *Tłumacz*. The word for *translator* was pronounced like the American expression "too much." Grażyna probably thought he'd been muttering about translating. "Do you like interpreting for the professor?" she asked. "Does he talk about America?"

It was an honor to be a translator, and Tomek knew he should feel gratitude. No one but he received pay for this work in Zakopane. Grażyna had been brought to

Widokówka to cook and clean, and she would return home with no more than she'd had when she'd left. But if he did not talk to somebody, he didn't know what he would do. Maybe this friend of his brother was the answer. "Grażyna, I am quitting."

She started to object, but he raised a finger to stop her. "I love translating. And to hear this man talk of literature, of our own poets, I could not have dreamed of this."

"But you will quit?" she asked. She twisted the wet rag over the hardwood floor, then rubbed the puddled spot.

"If this were all there is!" Tomek slapped the door in frustration. "But it is politics here as everywhere! Anna, Marek, and Stasiek believed they were coming to Zakopane to be taught by a native of Poland, not an American. They want nothing more than to write for the Information Bulletins of the TKN, but we still do not have the printing press Father B. promised to deliver. And Janek, when he bothers to attend, asks the professor hard questions I must soften in translation." He lowered his voice. "You more than anyone must know what Janek does in his absences. His black-market dealings will get us all—"

"*Shh!*" Grażyna looked both ways down the narrow hall, though Tomek was certain the others were all in the basement, waiting for him to start the class. "You do not know, Tomek, if Janek does these things."

She stopped. A door opened and shut, and footsteps sounded on the stairs above. Eva Lott trotted down the steps, her bare feet slapping wood as she pulled her sweater on over her shirt and blue jeans. When she reached their landing, her brown eyes, always round and bright as moons, flashed them a smile, the first he had seen from her.

"Did you see?" she shouted. "Mountains! Out the window! They're so . . . so . . . *piękne!*" She pronounced the last word, *beautiful*, precisely as a southern Pole would have.

Tomek stared, amazed, as, shoes in hand, she zipped past them and down the steps.

"What was that about?" Grażyna asked, staring after the American girl.

Tomek remembered the night of the house blessing. He laughed. "I do not think she believed that we are surrounded by the Tatras. We have had only gray skies since they arrived." He nodded to Grażyna and hurried down the stairs. He would have liked to get one more glimpse of Eva smiling like that, to see her face when she saw his country's tallest mountains for the first time.

When he reached the landing, he heard voices.

"Look! I told you! I don't know what you're saying." Eva Lott stood outside the open front door, gesturing wildly with her hands, which still held her shoes.

From where Tomek stood, he couldn't see who it was she was shouting at. But he could hear the man shouting back in Warsaw Polish: "Where is Janek Grzebieniowski? Why are you staying in this house with him?"

Tomek tiptoed closer until he saw the speaker, a gray-suited militia, not a local. His fist clenched and unclenched as Eva smiled at the officer, apparently unable to answer a single question.

"Did you see the mountains?" she asked him, her voice sweet as music. "You really should take a look. They're magnificent! And you never know when an ugly gray cloud will sweep back and hide them."

The militia screamed in Eva's face. "Are you a total idiot? Do you want I should haul you in for interrogation? You would like that maybe?"

Tomek ran outside and placed himself between the officer and Eva. "Get inside!" he whispered in English to Eva. "I will handle this."

"*You* get inside!" she whispered back. "I have it under control."

Tomek stepped back, forcing Eva to the doorstep. "May I help you, Commander?" he asked in Polish.

"Is she a fool? She wears no shoes. She is crazy!" he screamed.

Tomek shrugged. "Westerners." He tried to sound conspiratorial, but his heart throbbed in his throat, and his words had to squeeze out.

He sensed Eva, still standing behind him. She cleared her throat.

"I am seeking Janek Grzebieniowski. Do you know of him?"

Again Tomek shrugged. "Janek?" He shook his head. "I am on holiday. I am sorry. I have met few of the other lodgers."

The militia asked to see Tomek's papers, which he took from his wallet and handed over. This was exactly what he had feared would happen. If he got out of this, Tomek vowed, he would definitely quit.

Finally, the flush-faced man handed back the papers. Lowering his voice, he said, "While you are here, if you see this Janek, tell it to the police station in *centrum*, yes?"

Tomek nodded.

The officer sniffed, then wiped snot with the back of his hand. He gazed around Tomek for another look at Eva. It turned Tomek's stomach to watch the man almost salivate. "Good luck with that one, eh? Sexy little thing, but not worth the trip, as my papa used to say." He laughed, a sickly, guttural sound, then turned and made his way down the lane, his boots sloshing in the mud.

"He's a pig!" Eva exclaimed.

"Be quiet!" Tomek stared after the officer. He could still come back, ask one more question.

"I should have told him where to get off!" Eva fumed. She stormed around Tomek and shook her shoes at the militia. "If you hadn't come out when you did, I would have—!"

"You?" Tomek's fear emptied into anger. This American girl had no idea who it was she was dealing with. It frightened him to realize what might have happened to her if he hadn't come out when he did. "Why would you answer the door? *You?*"

"I didn't." Her face tightened, eyes narrowed to dagger tips. "I was going outside, and he was standing there. When he asked about Janek, I—"

"You should have left him there and come to get me! You could see he did not speak English." The pain in the pit of his stomach, the old ulcer he'd had two years before, gnawed at him now.

She actually grinned, as if she hadn't just risked her life and everyone else's around her. "Of course that idiot couldn't speak English! That's why *I* talked to him. I figured he'd get frustrated and go away. If I pretended I didn't understand or speak a word of Polish, he—"

"Ha! Pretended? That took great acting skill, no doubt!"

Eva drew herself up, and for a moment Tomek thought she would lunge at him. Instead, she walked calmly and gracefully past him, and inside. "No more skill than it would take for you to pretend you're human."

As the door slammed, Tomek gazed out at the Tatras and took in a deep breath of cold air. How he would love to climb the mountains surrounding Morskie Oko Lake right now. Let Eva translate, if she thought she could speak Polish. See how she fared in the lion's den Father B. had created in that basement. If it had not been for Tomek, Janek's activists would have come to blows with Oasis students like Krystyna and Andrzej, and Jacek, who only wanted to be a priest. After today they could find an interpreter who was also a referee. He'd had enough.

Too much!

One more breath, and he headed down to the basement, fifteen minutes late for a class that could not start without him.

Tomek heard the arguments before he reached the stairwell. He considered shouting down, "I quit!" in English and Polish and making a run for the mountains. But he would not do that to Father B. or to the professor.

"There he is!" Andrzej's whiskered face held the room's only grin for Tomek. Big wide-spaced teeth poked through a tiny goatee. His hat line still showed, where the too-tight beret had ridged his forehead. "Tomek, we are worse than nothing without you."

Professor Lott stood at one end of the long dining table turned study table, while the students sat on benches on either side. It was the house's only table, so they dragged it between the two basement rooms, the kitchen and this storage room they'd made into a classroom.

"Sorry, Tomek," called the professor. "I had Andrzej read from Adam Mickiewicz's *Dziady*, or *Forefathers' Eve*. I'm not sure what happened after that."

Tomek sifted through the angry voices as they all talked at once. Marek and Anna complained that the group should be writing about the Moscow trials instead of listening to a 150-year-old poem.

Jacek defended the professor, and Krystyna looked as if she might break down from the tension in the room.

"Tomek!" Professor Lott interrupted. "You have to translate everything they say."

"Yes. Yes, I am sorry." As he had done since the start, Tomek performed his balancing act—weeding out the negative comments to protect the professor, and rewording the professor's words so he would not stir up his students. It was the hardest thing Tomek had ever done. He would straighten out this one mess, finish this class, and be done with it.

For the next hour Tomek translated as Professor Lott made Mickiewicz come alive. Tomek lost himself in the words and their rhythm. He could have listened to the music of this poetry forever.

"*Shh!* Someone is coming!" Anna whispered to Tomek. She frowned up the basement steps.

The front door slammed. Tomek pictured the officer marching back, his militia buddies with him this time. He was glad Janek had not been around for three days.

"What's happening?" Professor Lott demanded.

But before Tomek could try to answer, footsteps sounded on the stairs.

Krystyna knocked over her empty tea glass and gasped as if it had broken.

Janek burst into the classroom, looking as if he had just been elected the first Polish president.

"What is it, Janek?" Anna asked.

"It is exactly what we have been waiting for!" he shouted. He clapped his hands together and did two steps of a Polish folk dance.

"What is it?" Professor Lott asked, smiling at this rare vision of a happy Janek.

"Tell the honorable professor," Janek said to Tomek, "that his class is going on a field trip." He waited for Tomek to translate, refusing to go on until he had.

"Professor Lott wants to know *where* this field trip is and what you intend for us to do, Janek," Tomek translated back to him.

Janek grinned, then lifted Anna off the ground and set her back down. "Tell him we are all off to Kraków tomorrow for a first-class Polish funeral!"

➻ 8 ⤙

"Eva, can't you put your clothes away?" Eva's dad sounded exasperated, and Eva suspected it had more to do with Janek than with her stuff on the floor of their tiny room. Her dad had come straight upstairs after class and told her about Janek's announcement of a funeral in Kraków. She knew her father didn't like surprises. Plus, she'd sensed Janek's control over some of the others. Dad wouldn't like that, either.

"At least keep your junk on your half of the room." With the toe of his shoe, he shoved her sweatshirt toward her bed.

Eva didn't see how she could stand another day sharing this *cell* with her father. "What *are* we—twelve?" she asked. "Should I get my jump rope and split the room officially, right down the middle?"

Her father sighed and breathed out a halfhearted laugh. "I know. I know."

He had always had the best posture of any human Eva had known. But after her mother died, her dad's shoulders seemed to grow even squarer. Eva had gone the other way. After Mom, Eva felt like her bones had dissolved, and her body didn't have anything to hang on to. Dad always harped at her to sit up straight, stand tall.

Yet a couple of weeks in Zakopane had taken the edges off Dad's shoulders. He stood in front of the wardrobe now, as slumped as she'd ever seen him. It made her want to cry.

Eva grabbed her inside-out sweatshirt and three bras off the floor and sat on her bed. Samson hopped into her lap and curled up, keeping one suspicious eye on his archenemy, Dad. Eva watched as her dad opened the wardrobe and fingered his two pairs of pants and three shirts.

"I don't have any idea what to wear to a funeral here," he said, not turning around.

Samson was licking her hand. The raspy tongue made her shiver, that or the near-freezing temperature of the room. The window above her bed had iced over inside and out. "I still don't get why Janek is so thrilled about going to a funeral," she said. "Does anybody even know the priest who died?"

"I think Andrzej heard him once," her dad answered, pulling down his green sweater from the six-inch-high shelf above the hanging bar. "And Jacek knows who he is.

But that's not the point. Funerals are political statements in Eastern Europe."

Her father turned to her, and Eva felt one of his long explanations coming on.

"You have to understand funerals in context here. They provide the only opportunity for large numbers of Poles to gather legally under one roof. There's a very good chance that Cardinal Wyszyński might attend, along with Wojtyła, Archbishop of Kraków."

By the time her dad finished his private lecture on funerals, he'd picked up steam and was packing his *torba,* a leather book bag he'd bought when he'd driven Father Blachnicki into Warsaw the week before. Their Renault was the only car in Father B.'s Oasis movement, as far as Eva could tell. In Zakopane, horse-drawn wagons outnumbered cars about ten to one.

The rest of the day, after kitchen duty, when she washed a million dishes, Eva did homework. After the first week of getting the correspondence-school system down, she hadn't needed her dad at all. She read the chapters, did the worksheets or wrote the essays, and made notes for tests. At the rate she was going, she'd be a month ahead of everybody when she finally got back to Chicago.

And she *would* get back to Chicago. While her dad had been teaching his classes in the mornings, Eva had been exploring Zakopane, searching for a way out. But the town, even though Poles vacationed there, was remote and cut off from the rest of the world. She'd concluded that her best chance of escape would be from a big city, where she could make her way to the airport and charge a plane ticket. She had a charge card. Her dad had given it to her in Chicago, for emergencies only.

Well, if this wasn't an emergency, nothing was.

Eva waited until nighttime to set her plan in motion. She would have to convince her father to take her with him to Kraków. Normally, it was next to impossible to convince Professor Raymond Lott of anything, especially if his daughter was the one doing the arguing. The trick was to make it seem like his idea.

Once in Kraków, it wouldn't be that hard to sneak off to the airport. By the time her dad realized she was gone, it would be too late. She'd be on her way to Chicago.

Eva waited for her dad to finish washing up. Neither of them ever took long, since everything—*everything*—had to be done without hot water. There was a bathtub, and a few times she'd boiled a pan of hot water on Pani Kurczak's stove, no small feat in itself. Those lukewarm baths had been her highlights in Poland. But most of the time, they sponged off with soap and cold water. Eva washed her hair in the sink, the cold water leaving her hair stiff and squeaky.

She propped up her book with one hand and scratched Samson's tummy with the other. The little dog lay on his back, paws in the air. Eva's only regret was that she couldn't take Samson with her. She'd gone over and over it, but there was no way she'd make it onto that plane with a dog. She would send for Samson the minute she got home.

Eva's dad would be only too glad to get rid of both of

them. She knew he loved her, that he'd be worried when he couldn't find her in Kraków. She didn't want him to panic. She'd call him the second she was safe and let him know.

But he didn't need her here. She was a liability to him. Nobody had even known she was coming to Zakopane. And the only students who didn't hate her were Krystyna, and maybe Grażyna, who at least tried to ask her about America. And Andrzej, of course, who liked everybody. Tomek would probably dance the polka when he found out she was gone.

The door opened and Eva's dad rushed in, his bare feet squeaking on the wood floor. His shoulders shook from the cold.

Eva pretended to read, as they did every night, her dad sitting in bed at a ninety-degree angle, his pillow propped against the wall, while Eva lay flat on her back, the book above her face as if she were sunning on the beach.

"I thought you finished *Pickwick Papers*," Dad said, climbing under his covers with a notebook and a volume of poetry.

"Yeah. Just rereading some of the funniest parts." Eva had surprised herself by actually enjoying the novels her dad had brought along. She'd run through her paperbacks in a week. This was her third Dickens novel. "So I guess attending the funeral is worth missing one class day, huh? What time are you leaving tomorrow, Dad?" To herself, she sounded casual, barely interested.

"Janek wants to leave at dawn. We'll take the bus, since everybody's going."

Eva sighed. "Everybody's going?"

"Not Pani Kurczak, of course."

"I see." She turned a page of *Pickwick Papers*.

Her dad seemed to be reading. Then he lowered his book. "You're not afraid to be alone, are you?"

"No." Her voice was flat, and she turned another page. He went back to his book.

"Maybe I can eat in the room. I don't think Pani Kurczak likes me in her kitchen by myself." *That's enough. Keep reading.* Eva calculated that this statement might have a twofold effect. How pitiful to envision his poor daughter sneaking food up to the room to keep out of the way. Plus her dad had never, not in all her eighteen years, allowed her to take food into her bedroom.

"So you'll be okay, then?" he asked.

"Sure." Was there a catch in her voice? Maybe drama club hadn't been a total waste.

"Because I just don't know what the funeral will be like," Dad muttered. Eva could almost hear his brain percolate, weighing pros and cons. He was thinking. The idea had occurred to him—she was sure of it.

It was all she could do not to jump in and argue, to make her case the way she always did. Instead, she sighed and turned another page.

"It could be dangerous," he continued. "On the other hand, these kinds of political funerals go on all the time in Poland."

"I understand," Eva said, setting down her book and turning to stare out the ice-crusted window.

"You'd probably hate the whole thing. The funeral's bound to be very long. And you'd find it very boring."

Eva felt like screaming, *As opposed to being here?* Instead, she managed, *"Me? I'd* find it boring?" She sat up, on the edge of her bed, and faced him. "You mean I'm invited? I didn't think any of your students liked me enough to want me to tag along."

A wave of empathy passed across her father's face, so sincere, so sad, she almost felt guilty. Almost. "Of course they like you, Eva! And I'm sure they'd be happy to have you come along to Kraków if—"

"You're kidding!" She smiled as if he'd just informed her she'd been nominated homecoming queen. "Then, yeah. I wouldn't want them to think I don't want to go with them. Sure. I'll come." She got up and walked to the wardrobe.

"Well . . . I don't . . . I mean . . . it could take all day and most of the night," her dad warned.

"Better have my secretary clear my schedule then." She turned and smiled at Dad, then searched the wardrobe for socks. They'd washed their clothes two days ago, in the same sink Eva used to wash her hair, with the same cold water. But the room was so cold that it took days for things to dry. She'd probably have to go with dirty and dry, over clean and damp.

Eva sat on the bus to Kraków, next to Krystyna. Through the window she watched the most beautiful snowcapped peaks stretch jagged fingers toward the blue sky. At least she'd stayed long enough to see the mountains. Smoke rose from every chimney as they bounced out of Zakopane.

Eva's dad and Tomek sat in front of them, deep in conversation over some poet named Tadeusz Różewicz. Eva couldn't stop thinking about Samson. She would have given anything to take him back with her, to have the little dog curled on her lap right now.

In the middle of the night, she'd pulled on the Peter Frampton shirt Matt had given her, just so she wouldn't leave it behind. But she'd forgotten to take other things, like her mother's earrings. They were Mom's favorite pair—long, silver, and dangly.

Eva remembered her mother dancing in the kitchen between fridge and oven, Beach Boy music blaring from the radio she kept on the sill. And the earrings jingling, gyrating with a life of their own. Now they sat back at Widokówka, in the corner of the wardrobe.

"You miss your friends from America very much, yes?" Krystyna asked. Kystyna's Polish was the easiest to understand. She was one of the few Eva had talked with in Polish for more than a couple of words. Sometimes Andrzej came to the room to talk to her dad, and Eva had to play interpreter. But the others, like Tomek, assumed she couldn't speak Polish, or understand. This had actually given her a kind of spy status. One morning she'd eavesdropped on an argument between Anna and Janek. Anna reminded Eva of Mel's Persian cat—beautiful, graceful, but always ready to scratch the unsuspecting. Anna had been complaining about the fact that they were being taught by an American. She liked it even less that the American professor had brought along "his spoiled American daughter."

Eva had expected at least some of the people to speak

English. Most of them, as it turned out, did speak at least two languages—just not English. Krystyna had explained that students were only allowed to study Russian in school, or possibly German. English had to be learned "under the table," or as a third or fourth language in upper-level studies.

Krystyna, eyebrows raised, was staring at her, waiting for an answer.

"I do miss my friends," Eva admitted, leaning back in the cold seat. The bus jostled them into each other at every bump, but Krystyna didn't seem to notice.

"Tell me about them, your friends of America." Krystyna smiled up at her so hard her eyes disappeared. "Please?" She reminded Eva of Matt's little sister, Sarah, who'd do anything to get another story out of Eva, usually stories Eva's mom had passed down to her.

Eva smiled back at Krystyna, who had been kind to her since her arrival at Widokówka. Eva had to admit, she herself hadn't always returned the kindness. She wished she'd at least tried with Krystyna. Maybe now, if she talked about her friends, Krystyna would understand when everybody found out she'd run back to the USA. Maybe Krystyna wouldn't hold it against her.

"Krystyna," she said, turning in the bus seat, tucking one leg under her, "let me tell you about Matt . . ."

Half a dozen times during her conversation with Krystyna, Tomek had glanced at them over the bus seat. Eva had pretended not to notice. The bus jerked to a stop and let out its breath in a cloud of exhaust.

Her dad stood up and stretched in the aisle. "We'll take the train from here," he explained, yawning. "Should put us in before noon."

Eva should have felt tired, too. But she had too much adrenaline pumping. She could almost smell Chicago.

⇥ 9 ⇤

No one fainted from surprise when the Nowy Targ train arrived over an hour late. But by the time they realized it had come in on the wrong track, they had to run to catch it.

Still, by noon they were pulling into Kraków to the squeal of metal on metal, brakes on tracks. Eva's dad had slipped into the seat with Eva when Krystyna left their car to find Grażyna. He'd fallen asleep immediately, head crooked against the torn backrest, his mouth open. For the first time, Eva noticed that his hair was thinning in back, a white scalp peeking through.

She shuddered, remembering the day she'd noticed her mother's hair falling out, clumps lying in the wastebasket. Eva hadn't been able to grasp the whole idea of a *cancer* you couldn't even see. But this white-gray scalp instead of shiny auburn hair had made the threat so real, she'd run to the bathroom and vomited.

"Dad?" She put her hand on his head and felt the coarse hair, noticing lines around his eyes and mouth. Eva hadn't counted on missing him, not really, not very much. She didn't think she would have if he'd left her in Chicago weeks ago. At least now she understood, a little, anyway, why he'd wanted to come here. He really did believe in freeing Poland by teaching people to write the truth and appreciate the writing of others. She almost envied him that.

"We're here, Dad."

She'd write him a note, a great note, saying all the things she'd never said to him here, that she wasn't mad at him anymore. He *had* to come to Poland, just like she *had* to leave, to go home.

Dad jerked, then sat up fast. "Guess I might have dozed off a minute. Are we here?"

The train gave a jolt and let out a gasp.

Eva and her dad waited until the rest of their group got off. The students had agreed to split up and meet in Nowa Huta, a suburb of Kraków, where the funeral would take place that evening.

As they climbed down the platform steps and onto the out station, her dad whispered, "I hate to admit I'm looking forward to this funeral as much as Janek is, but I am. It's at the Arka, one of the top sites I wanted to see while we're in Poland. In case we get separated, Eva, just ask how to get to the Church of Our Lady of Poland. I'm not sure how that translates, though. Tomek says we take the number-ten tram to Nowa Huta."

They crossed through the station and entered a tunnel,

like undergrounds back home. Slogans covered the dank walls, scrawled in red paint. Eva made out several that said the same thing: REMEMBER SEPTEMBER 17!

"What was September seventeenth?" she asked her dad.

But Tomek, walking up behind them, answered, "The date of the Soviet invasion of Poland."

He fell in with them, and Eva tried not to show her irritation. Now she not only had to lose her dad, she had to worry about Tomek.

"Poland has suffered through Septembers," her father said. "'The unmentionable odour of death / Offends the September night . . .'"

Tomek continued, in the same somber tone Eva's dad had spoken in. "'Defenceless under the night / Our world in stupor lies.'"

Her dad seemed surprised. "You know Auden?"

"'September 1, 1939,' written after Germany invaded our country. It is one of my favorites."

Eva looked from her father to Tomek, seeing them as if she were in Chicago, watching them from the other side of a television screen. Already her dad had a connection with Poland, and Poland with him. He and Tomek were joined together in some way she and her dad never had been and simply couldn't be now.

Ahead, near the tunnel exit, a dark-skinned black-haired boy, who must have been about six or seven, sat cross-legged against the cold tiled wall. Sad deep-toned music floated through the tunnel, drowning out footsteps and voices. He was playing an accordion, pushing and pulling at it with one hand while the other hand made the tiny keyboard sound like a grand piano. An old man dropped coins into the boy's battered upside-down hat.

Eva stopped as they reached him. It was unbelievable that the music could come from this child, from that chipped, worn accordion. He had the biggest, darkest eyes she had ever seen.

They came out onto a cobblestone street beside a barren park. Her dad reached into his *torba* and pulled out a handful of bills, which he handed to Eva. "You should have some złoty of your own. You might see a good souvenir for Mel or somebody."

"Thanks." She wished he hadn't passed the money in front of Tomek, who probably thought all Americans were filthy rich, already. But the money would come in handy. For the plane ticket, she had her secret weapon—the MasterCard. But there might be other expenses getting to the airport.

"We have time if you want me to show you Kraków," Tomek offered.

The only part of Kraków Eva wanted to be shown was the exit. And Tomek couldn't help with that one.

"Thanks, Tomek," Eva's dad said. "That would be great. But first, I'm starving. Think you could find us a good place for lunch?"

"That is not a problem," Tomek replied.

Eva saw her chance. "I'm too excited to eat now. You guys go ahead, though. I'll meet up with you later."

Her dad shook his head. "I don't know about that, Eva. We're not sure what's going to happen in Kraków today, with the funeral and everybody coming to hear the cardinals."

It was true that the streets were much more crowded than when she and her dad had driven into the city and waited for Tomek. But it was still not even close to downtown Chicago on a regular day.

"I'll be careful." She tried to keep her voice down, keep it casual. She might blow the whole thing. She smiled at both of them. "Besides, I'm going to want a lot more shopping time than you guys are going to be able to handle. Maybe I should just meet you at the funeral. I could take the number-ten tram, right?"

"Wrong! Absolutely not!" Dad looked around, probably to see if people were watching.

Eva had known he wouldn't go for that one, so now she tried something with better odds. "Yeah. You're probably right. Okay. So you two get something to eat. I'll do some shopping and meet you at the lunch place. That sound good?"

Her dad turned to Tomek. "Is there a place to eat right around here?"

Tomek pointed out a cafeteria that from the outside looked a hundred times worse than Eva's school cafeteria at home. "Their food is good and priced well," he said.

"I'll give you one hour, Eva," her dad finally conceded.

"Three?" Eva suggested.

"Two! And that's final. And don't go far, okay?"

She stood on tiptoes and kissed his forehead. It would have to do for a good-bye. "Thanks." She had to go. She turned quickly and walked away.

"Two hours, Eva!" her dad called after her. "Don't make us wait!"

Eva knew better than to look back. He'd be fine. Better without her. She'd leave him a message at the airport somehow, so he wouldn't have to wait until she arrived in Chicago to find out what happened to her.

Two hours. That's all she'd have to get to the Kraków airport. Once she was inside that airport, she'd be okay. Her dad wouldn't think to look for her there, not right away.

Eva forced herself to walk slowly. She knew her dad well enough to suspect he'd still be standing there, watching to see where she was going. She headed for the central shopping square at the end of the street and stepped inside the arched stone arcade. They had walked past the square on their way to Wawel Castle to meet Tomek. It seemed impossible that only weeks, and not years, had passed since then.

In the arcade, vendors called to her from every stall. She stopped at one and picked up the finely carved wooden boxes and chess sets. If she had more time, she might have bought gifts for Mel and Matt.

But she didn't have time. And as soon as she was sure her dad couldn't see her any longer, she took off running down the rocky streets of Kraków.

➤➤ 10 ◄◄

Eva ran past high-spired churches with ugly animals carved into them. People stared as she raced past them. She had to stop running. She suspected the airport must be on the outskirts of the city, because she hadn't seen a single plane flying over. But for all she knew, she might be going in the wrong direction.

An older man in a corduroy beret and a green coat was walking in her direction.

"Excuse me, please," she said in her best Polish. "Which way is the airport?"

He smiled at her and rattled off something in what Eva thought was German. Before she could tell him she wasn't German, he patted her head and walked on.

She asked four more people and couldn't understand their answers, or they didn't get the question. Their Polish sounded different from Krystyna's, more complex.

Finally, she realized that Krystyna had been speaking pidgin Polish, simplifying the language for her. And she'd never even let on. Instead, she'd constantly praised Eva's Polish. Eva wished she'd known. She kept walking. At least she had to be getting farther and farther from the cafeteria. She looked at every sign, hoping to see an airport symbol. At a kiosk, she rummaged through maps, searching for a guide to the city. But everything was in Polish, and nothing showed signs of an airport.

She figured she'd been gone an hour, half of her *safe* time before they'd start looking for her. Her stomach ached from hunger, and she still didn't know where the airport was.

She had to think. Passing the empty window of a butcher shop, she stopped and stared in. The shelves looked as barren as in Zakopane.

In the reflection of the glass, Eva saw a short-haired teenaged-looking girl, with no hat and only a thin quilted jacket. The girl smiled at Eva's reflection in the glass.

Eva turned around and asked in Polish, "Which way is the airport?"

The girl brightened and asked in very precise English, "You are English?"

"Yes! I mean, American. Do you speak English?" Eva could have hugged her.

"I have never met American," she answered.

Eva stuck out her hand. "Eva Lott. Thank you for speaking English!"

The girl shifted her bag to one arm and shook Eva's hand. "I am Gosia."

It was a minute before Eva stopped shaking Gosia's hand and returned it to her. "Listen, I really need to get to the airport and get a flight to the United States. Can you help me? I could take a taxi, but I haven't seen one. Is it very far?"

The girl smiled, showing white teeth. "There is no airport in the city. Far outside of Kraków, yes. But no airplanes to your country."

"What? Wait. How can they not fly to America?" Never once had she considered the possibility that a huge city like Kraków wouldn't have a flight home. She felt like an idiot.

"You must to take train to Warsaw. The airport here closes some days."

Warsaw? Eva tried to pull herself together. It was a setback, no doubt about it. But why couldn't she take the train to Warsaw? It meant finding her way back to the train station. But if they'd take the credit card, she could do it. And if they didn't, she had the Polish money her dad had given her.

"Thank you—," Eva started. But Gosia had vanished. Eva glanced up and down the street, but the girl was gone. And Eva hadn't even told her how great her English was.

She tried to remember how to get back to the train station—without passing the lunch place, where her father and Tomek were waiting. Falling in with a group of pedestrians, she joined the ranks of women in scarves and men in caps, walking without talking. In the street, an occasional car chugged by, each one gray and small.

She thought she recognized a side street, so she left her Polish pedestrian pack and turned down the narrow, stone street. But the road stopped looking familiar and opened onto a busy *ulica* she was sure she'd never seen before.

Eva wandered past a jewelry store and another kiosk until she came to an Orbis office, a branch of the official government travel bureau. She stared in the window at the travel agents, who looked like uniformed airline stewardesses. The people in Orbis could tell her how to get to the train station. But would it be too risky to ask them? They'd spot her accent and might start asking questions she didn't want to answer.

In the glass of the Orbis window, Eva could see across the street to a row of dingy brick buildings. Something there caught her attention—letters on the window of one of the buildings. The reflection flipped the letters backward, but there was no mistaking the middle ʒs. She wheeled around and started to cross the street for a better look. It couldn't be what she thought, what she hoped.

A hand grabbed her shoulder and pulled her back, just as a tram whizzed in front of her from the right. Eva watched, stunned, as the brown metal tram jostled on the rail. It had been a close call. She hadn't expected anything to come from that direction.

"Thank you so much—! I mean, *dʒiękuję! Dʒiękuję bardʒo!*"

The woman let go of Eva's coat as if it were filthy. She looked like one of the shrunken apple dolls Mel had brought back from her trip to the Ozarks. A shriveled chin stuck out from under a flowered head-scarf, with no more than a line for a mouth.

Shaking her finger, the Polish woman muttered, *"Zwariowana Amerykanka!" Crazy American.*

"Perceptive as well as charming," Eva said in English, returning the woman's scowl with a hearty smile. She saluted her and dashed across the street.

No way! On the smudged window, in cracked, yellow letters was the word: PIZZA. Visions of Pizza Hut, extra cheese, sausage, and black olives, danced in her brain. A handwritten menu was stuck in the corner of the window. Halfway down the list of unidentifiable foods were the words POLISH PIZZA.

Eva convinced herself that the only logical course of action was to get a quick bite of pizza before heading to Warsaw. She had to keep up her strength. She could ask the waiter how to get to the train station. And anyway, if she raced to the station right now, she might run into her dad.

One step inside the dark restaurant told her this was no Pizza Hut. Most of the half-dozen customers, all men, seemed to be drinking instead of eating, one hand wrapped around liquor bottles with no labels.

She took the table by the window, brushing crumbs from the wooden seat before sitting down.

A waiter appeared but offered no menu. He seemed to be waiting for her order.

"Pizza?" Eva asked.

She waited for the waiter to tell her what kinds they had. Instead, he nodded and scurried back to the kitchen.

So what? She'd go for olives or sausage or onions or pepperoni or anything, so long as it was pizza.

While she waited, Eva wondered how much this would cost. She stuck her hand in her pocket and felt the wad of Polish paper money, hoping it was enough. Her dad had been thoughtful to give her Polish money of her own.

Outside, the day grew grayer. She tried not to think of her father. Just about now, he'd be glancing toward the cafeteria door, irritated but not worried, not yet.

A woman walked by the window, and for the flash of an instant, Eva thought it was her mother. Not that the woman looked anything like Eva's mother. She didn't. It might have been the way she moved her arms as she walked or something about her hair. Eva rarely knew what triggered these painful Mom sightings. But each time, a familiar pain sliced through her as the hope dissolved and she realized that, of course, it wasn't Mom.

Everybody had said that time would heal and the pain would diminish. But it hadn't been like that for Eva. It was true that she didn't think about Mom every minute, the way she had those first weeks. But when she did, the pain was just as intense as it had been at her mother's funeral. It was waiting around corners—in the movement of an elbow, the wave of a hand, a glimpse of auburn hair.

The waiter returned, holding a silver tray high in one hand. The tray had a large, round silver cover just like Eva had seen in movies about rich families. She tried to get a whiff of the pizza and guess what kind it was before the waiter removed the lid. But it wasn't a smell she recognized.

Eva could hardly stand it. The waiter lifted the lid dramatically and set the platter in front of her.

She stared at it. Thick tomato paste covered a thin, hard crust. There was no sign of cheese anywhere. And on top, instead of pepperoni, tiny fish lay on their sides, each with one eye staring up at her. Sardines, swimming in a pool of red.

Eva felt her stomach flop like a dying fish. She couldn't pretend to eat this. She couldn't even sit there and look at it or smell it.

"Check!" She swallowed and thought she could taste something fishy. "I want my bill."

The waiter didn't understand. The old men at the next table turned to watch.

Eva tried charades, acting out paying. She drew a bill on the tablecloth then held up her wad of Polish money. Finally, the phrase from her Berlitz class came back to her. *"Poproszę o rachunek!"*

The waiter nodded, then disappeared behind swinging doors. When he returned, he placed a slip of paper facedown on the tablecloth.

Eva turned it over. It looked like pure scribble, with nothing but consonants. She held it to the light, but it was no use. She couldn't read it, not even the odd-shaped numbers.

She reached into her pocket, took out a handful of bills, and smoothed them out on the table. They looked less real than Monopoly money.

Terrified that they'd stop her, scream at her that she hadn't left enough, she pulled out the rest of the paper złoty and piled it next to the smoothed bills. This was all she had, and she hoped it was enough, especially since she hadn't eaten a bite.

As Eva stood to leave, the waiter rushed back to her table. She felt as if she'd been caught shoplifting again. Only this time, the idea terrified her.

He picked up the bills, glanced at Eva, stared back at the bills.

She grabbed her coat and stepped away, bumping the table behind her. She had to get out of there. If she owed them money, it wasn't her fault. She hadn't even eaten anything.

The waiter snatched her coat out of her hands.

"I'm sorry!" she cried.

He held up the coat and nodded for her to step into it. *"Dziękuję!"* he exclaimed. *"Dziękuję bardzo!"*

Thank you very much? Eva slipped into her coat. She must have left enough to cover the pizza. And the tip.

The bartender ran over and shook her hand. Then a man with a chef's hat came to her table and bowed. All of them looked like they'd just won the lottery.

How much had she left them, anyway?

Eva nodded and made her way outside. As she walked past the restaurant, someone tapped on the window from inside. Eva looked up to see the waiter and bartender waving wildly at her behind the big window.

The sky had clouded over. An icy wind blew in from the west. And Eva Lott had never felt so alone. She didn't know where she was. Or what she was doing.

Turning up her collar against the wind, Eva took off,

walking fast, hoping she was retracing her steps to the train station.

"Eva!" A man was yelling from across the street.

Eva didn't look. He couldn't mean her.

"Eva!"

Footsteps sounded from the street, coming closer. She looked up to see Tomek Muchowiecki leap to the curb. He planted himself directly in front of her. "So where do you think you are going?"

⤜ 11 ⤛

It took Eva a minute to answer him. Tomek frowned at her, his hair blowing in fierce gusts of wind.

"I . . . I'm on my way back," she finally managed.

Tomek cocked his head and stared at her, looking like he didn't buy it.

"Okay. You got me. I'm lost. Satisfied?" It was exactly what he'd wanted to hear. She could see his mouth twitch, trying not to smile. "And nobody understood my Polish when I asked them how to get back."

That did it. Tomek got his superior look.

"I'll bet Dad's going nuts."

"It is okay," Tomek said. "We have met Father Blachnicki in the *bar mleczny*, the cafeteria. He has need of your father, and they have gone ahead to Nowa Huta."

So her dad hadn't worried about her at all. She knew it was unreasonable, but the realization still stung.

Tomek stuck his hands in his pockets and turned away from the wind. "You and I will follow to meet them there."

If she hadn't run into Tomek, she could have made it to Warsaw and been on the plane before her dad had even realized she was gone. Suddenly, Eva felt the cold, her hunger . . . and she had to go to the bathroom.

"So," Tomek said. "Is there something you wish to see or do before we leave Kraków for Nowa Huta?"

"Yes, there is, Tomek. I'd like to go to the john."

He frowned. "John?"

"Powder my nose? Skip to my loo?"

Tomek shook his head. "I do not understand. Powder your nose? Cosmetics?"

As much as she enjoyed Tomek's obvious confusion, she really did have to go. "A bathroom, Tomek. I want to go—no, I *have* to go to the bathroom."

Tomek's face flushed bright red. He had a good face, with a broad forehead, firm chin, and deep-set brown eyes. It was the kind of face you might find on a marble sculpture, classic. It almost surprised Eva to see Tomek this way now, nearly as much as it surprised her to realize she had barely seen him at all before now.

Without a word, Tomek led her straight back to the sardine-pizza restaurant.

"I can't go in here!" she protested.

"They have restroom," he assured her. "I will go with you." He stepped inside.

"Great. That makes it so much better." Eva trailed in after Tomek, hiding her face by pretending to cough.

Tomek pointed down a set of wide stairs, and she

took them, following the arrow down to the *toaleta*. She pushed on the door with a silhouette of a female on it and slammed into what felt like a Russian tank. Eva looked up into the bulldog face of a large woman in a white uniform. With a Jolly Green Giant stance, the stout woman guarded the entrance to the toilets. Her head reminded Eva of a Volkswagen bug—with the doors open.

The woman barked something that sounded like the Polish word for *give* and pointed to a small glass plate on her table. The plate held half a dozen tiny silver and gold Polish coins. But Eva only had an American five-dollar bill in her purse. She held it out to the woman.

"Nie!" bellowed the woman, refusing the bill.

Eva had to go to the bathroom. "Come on," she mumbled in Polish, looking through her pockets for anything. "Isn't this bill worth about a truckload of those stupid coins?"

The giant held up her palm, traffic-cop style.

Eva turned on her heels and raced back upstairs.

"We can go now," Tomek said.

"No. We cannot go now. I have to pay for the privilege of using the dirtiest bathroom I've ever seen. And the lovely woman downstairs has a serious problem with dollars."

Tomek reached into his inner coat pocket and pulled out a small leather change purse. He held out two silver coins in his big rough palm.

She felt like a beggar. But she had to go. Picking up the coins, she muttered, "Thanks."

Eva tore down the stairs, handed over the coins, and

was permitted to pass—just like on the troll's bridge in Three Billy Goats Gruff.

The restroom was filthy enough to make her wonder what the giant did to earn her money. Eva was about ready to use the toilet when she realized there was no toilet paper.

She'd have to face the troll lady again.

"Toilet paper?" Eva pointed toward the stall. "*Nie* toilet paper."

Troll lady, who was now sitting behind the table, reading a magazine, couldn't be bothered to look up.

Eva had seen the small squares of brown paper stacked on the woman's table—the Polish version of toilet paper. "*Proszę, Pani?*"

Troll woman belched.

Eva reached across the table to get some paper herself.

"*Nie!*" The woman spouted more angry Polish words that Eva figured meant no way are you getting any toilet paper, turkey. Then she slumped back in her chair and thumped a plate of coins next to the paper.

"You have got to be kidding! I have to *buy* the paper?"

But she didn't have any more coins. She'd put both of Tomek's coins in the plate. And she knew better than to ask for one back. Eva stared at the troll. "You are the ugliest, rudest person I've ever met in my whole life. I will purchase your gross paper and use your gross toilet and get out of your gross country as fast as I can." She said it in English, in mock sweetness, a warm smile plastered to her face.

At the top of the stairs, Tomek stood exactly where she'd left him.

Eva took a deep breath. "I have to buy the toilet paper."

She could have sworn Tomek grinned as he handed her a small gold coin.

Barely able to hold it in another second, she ran back down and bought her toilet paper. "Now," she said in sweet English, "I just want to do my business and get out of your kingdom."

But the troll woman stuck out her arm to block the entrance. She held out her hand and rubbed her thumb and index finger together.

"You're kidding!" Eva screamed. "I didn't even use your old toilet last time!"

The woman was unmoved. She outweighed Eva by a hundred pounds. And Eva *really* had to go now—and go quick.

She ran back upstairs, held out her hand to Tomek, got two more coins, and raced back down with them. At last the troll woman was pleased, and Eva was allowed to pass.

She finished what she came for, then splashed water on her face and walked upstairs. "Don't say a word," she warned Tomek, as she kept moving toward the exit.

They were halfway to the door when the waiter came running to them. He signaled the bartender, who leaped over the bar, waving and calling at Eva to come and sit down.

Eva shoved Tomek to the door, waving behind her at the men, who followed them, begging them to come back inside.

"What is that all about?" Tomek asked as they walked away. "They were pleading with you to stay with them, to dine with them."

Eva gave him her sweetest troll-lady smile. "Well, Tomek, in case you haven't noticed, I'm a big hit in Poland."

The sun had been swallowed by gray clouds and smoke by the time the number-ten tram to Nowa Huta pulled in. Tomek and Eva were lucky to make it before the door shut on a mass of people waiting, some of them waving tickets.

For the whole ride, Eva's face was crushed into Tomek's chest as he held on to the ceiling bar. She didn't have to hold on. She couldn't budge. Twice she looked up at Tomek and found him staring at her before he looked quickly away.

When the door swished open, they were swept out of the bus by the crowd. Eva had never seen so many people, not even after a St. Patrick's Day parade in downtown Chicago. Like a school of fish caught in a river current, the crowd moved in the same direction, taking Tomek and Eva with them. Eva couldn't see anything except shoulders and backs and arms.

"This way!" Tomek shouted, taking her arm and

pulling her through the hordes of people. "I know a man!" He led her out of the masses and up a hill. He moved so fast she could hardly catch her breath. Icy air chilled her lungs.

"Just a minute, Tomek!" she cried, pulling her arm away and leaning over, her hands braced on her knees until she could breathe regularly. She stood up and turned to gaze back at the crowd.

Throngs of people moved steadily, coughed out of buses and trams, swarming toward what looked like a giant wooden ark. Though the night was black, thousands of tiny lights burned around the building, blinking like a second layer of stars.

"Is that the church?" She'd expected a stone cathedral like the ones in Kraków. This one looked like a tremendous boat, plopped down from the sky. Crowds were already lining the grounds outside of the ark as if, expecting a flood, everybody wanted a seat inside.

Tomek moved closer to Eva. She felt him touch her shoulder, then pull away. "Do you not know about the ark church at Nowa Huta?"

She shook her head, unable to look away from the shimmering light of the thousands of candles below.

"The Soviet Union built steel mills here to dilute Kraków's student and professional population. Nowa Huta was to be a model of Communism, a churchless 'workers' paradise.' The government did not allow a church built in this suburb. They wanted the Communist laborers to clash with traditional and religious Kraków.

Instead, labor and religion united. All the townspeople—rich, poor, doctors, steelworkers—waged a twenty-year battle for a church. Across Poland, people took up this battle. Peasants sent what they could from harvest. Village churches sent altars and chalices. Visitors left their jewelry. And out of this gray concrete desert was built the Church of Our Lady of Poland, the Arka."

"And that's where the funeral is?" Eva asked. She was touched by this unexpected tenderness in Tomek. He wasn't just spouting facts to her. This was *his* story, his country, and he was sharing it with her.

"Yes." He started back up the hill.

"Why are we going this way, then?" she shouted.

"There will be no seats inside the church. My friend will provide us with the next-best thing."

Eva struggled to keep up. They reached the top of the hill. On the other side, concrete factories spread out as far as Eva could see, their flaming smokestacks lighting the ugly blocks and barrels. The stench of burning sulfur hung over them. But across from the factories, looking as out of place as the Arka, was a small plot of land, a farm the size of a city playground.

Tomek and Eva made their way to the tiny farm, passing hay mounds that guarded a tiny wooden shack at the end of the plowed field.

A rail-thin, nearly toothless farmer ran out of his house to greet them.

"Piotrek, this is my friend Eva," Tomek said in Polish.

Eva doubted he would have used the word *friend* if he'd known she could understand. She was glad he didn't know, that even for this one night he might think of her as a *przyjaciółka*, a friend.

Piotrek hugged Tomek and bowed to Eva.

She returned the bow. *"Dobry wieczór."*

"Piotrek is one of a handful of farmers fighting to farm in Nowa Huta," Tomek explained in English.

Piotrek stepped back inside his shack and returned with a blanket and two chunks of brown bread.

Eva thanked him and started in on her bread while Tomek and his friend hooked up a horse, which was as skinny as his master, to a hay wagon, half loaded with hay. She climbed onto the wagon flat, and Tomek took the seat next to his friend.

As Piotrek drove his horse straight down the hill, Eva had to hold on so she wouldn't bounce out of the wagon. They passed hundreds of people, pilgrims of all ages. Eva scanned the crowd for her dad or any of the others from his class, but it was useless.

As they got closer, music drifted out of the church, a droning without instruments. It grew louder and louder, picked up by the crowd and tossed backward to others. The wagon serpentined to the far side of the ark church, where a break in the mass of bodies opened up. Piotrek urged his horse all the way to the back wall, then jumped down.

Tomek turned to Eva. "He knows a hole we can see through." He jumped down and stood next to the wagon, his arms outstretched.

Here behind the church it was so dark that Eva couldn't see the ground. But she could see Tomek. She glanced around, then jumped, eyes closed.

He caught her before her feet touched the ground, and he held her that way for a fraction of a second longer than he had to. Eva felt sure of it. Slowly he set her down. Her breath caught in her throat. Something inside of her shuddered.

Tomek walked to the other side of the wagon, and for minutes he and Piotrek talked low and laughed often.

Eva didn't even try to understand what they were saying. Instead, she deliberately turned her thoughts to Chicago—to her home, where Matt was waiting for her. She would have to start all over with her escape plans. But at least nobody was aware of her failed attempt today. Next time, she could go straight to Warsaw and—

"Tutaj!" Piotrek pointed to where Eva could peek between two of the boards. His jacket sleeve flapped around his bony wrist. Up close Eva could see his eyes—*smiling eyes,* her mother would have called them, clear and bright as the stars.

Through the crack in the church, she saw an altar, the back of the priests, and the congregation, most of them kneeling, without spaces between them. Some held candles, some sang, and many were crying. In front was what looked more like a crate than a casket. But the plain pine box was covered with a garden of flowers and surrounded by candles.

Piotrek told them Wojtyła couldn't make it to the funeral. But for the next hour, they listened as Cardinal Wyszyński, the man her dad had most wanted to see, spoke to the crowds:

"Our brother did not die in vain, for he lived to nurture his Poland before God Almighty, to demand respect for all Poles, independence, civil rights . . . We must have freedom of the press, freedom . . ."

Eva made out enough to understand that his sermon went far beyond a normal funeral speech.

She scanned the crowd until she spotted her father, sitting next to Andrzej, near the back.

"Did you hear that?" Tomek asked.

Piotrek nodded.

Eva hadn't heard anything except the cardinal's shouts for freedom.

Then she heard it, a rumbling, like a truck's racing engine. Voices rose from the surrounding hill, shouts that sounded angry or scared.

"What is it?" she asked Tomek.

He frowned, then exchanged a worried glance with Piotrek. "They're coming," he said quietly.

"Who?" Eva shouted, images of Scarface and Furry Hat flashing in front of her.

Wisps of fog floated across the churchyard. Then through the mist came a lone boy, running and shouting. The crowd standing outside the church began to murmur. Heads turned. Someone screamed.

Behind the boy, legs, boots, and arms poked through the fog. Footsteps snapped on concrete. Regular, loud steps, rows of boots marching in time. Lines of soldiers advanced, rifles aimed.

"The militia!" Eva cried. "Tomek!"

The roaring grew loud, drowning out the shouts of the crowd. There was a sound like metal scraping concrete. Then onto the church grounds rolled a tank. Eva had only seen tanks in movies, but there was no mistaking it. A second tank came from the east and another from the west, their long guns waving back and forth as if looking for someone to kill.

⇥ 12 ⇤

Tomek watched the militia break up the crowds below them. A woman lunged to get out of the way of a charging tank and fell inches from its path. Tomek wanted to run at the tank, to jump on top of it and beat it with his fists. This is how they had taken his brother. The militia had forced guns and tanks through a sea of human life, leaving waves of death and sorrow that did not go away, not ever. He imagined Tadeusz hearing the rumble of tanks, the shots from machine guns, the screams of terror.

"Tomek, we must leave!" Piotrek shouted. His horse reared in the harness. Piotrek yanked on the reins to keep the mare from bolting.

"Take Eva!" Tomek shoved her toward Piotrek.

Eva backed away from them. "I won't go! Not without Dad! Tomek, he's in there!"

Tomek wanted her out of there. More than anything, he wanted Eva safe. He went to her and shook her by the shoulders. "Go! I will look after your father!"

She stared back at him, not flinching. "I won't leave, Tomek."

"Eva—!" She was the most stubborn person he had ever met. There was no use talking to her. "Wait here!"

Piotrek struggled with his horse. "Tomek, be careful!" he yelled after him.

Tomek moved around the church the long way, keeping close to the building. Frightened men and women, some clutching their children, streamed by as he forced his way through the stampeding mob rushing from the Arka. A small boy in a torn blue jacket stumbled and fell at Tomek's feet. Tomek scooped up the boy and scanned the crowd until he spotted the mother, arms outstretched, her face contorted as she cried out for her son. He handed the boy to her and kept pushing toward the church.

"Tomek!" Anna threw her arms around him. "They've got Tymoteusz and Marek and I don't know who else! Have you seen Janek?"

A stout man bumped into them, sending Tomek and Anna crashing hard against the church.

"Go through the field, Anna!" Tomek shouted. "Janek can take care of himself."

She nodded, bent her head, and joined the fleeing masses.

Tomek made it to the entrance of the church. Militia pointed rifles at the crowd still pushing to get out. They poked their rifle butts at random.

He backed up to the nearest window, then looked inside. Chairs were toppled. A small fire burned next to the coffin. Cardinal Wyszyński held his ground in front, shouting at the soldiers.

Then Tomek spotted Professor Lott in the middle of the sanctuary. He was shielding Krystyna, who was crouched on the floor.

Tomek didn't know what to do. If he tried to push past the militia at the entrance, he would be arrested. He glanced at the nearest soldier guarding the door. Something about the man looked familiar. Tomek knew him. They had been children together in Brzegi. He had not seen Jurek for years, though he had heard his old friend had joined the army.

It was his only chance. Tomek, his back against the church wall, inched his way to Jurek.

"You there!" Jurek yelled, raising his rifle at Tomek.

Tomek stared down the barrel of the gun. "Jurek? I am Tomek Muchowiecki. From Brzegi."

Jurek didn't lower the rifle. His face looked more like his father's, though he had not grown so tall. "Tomek?"

"Jurek, I must enter the church. There is someone I must get to safety."

Tomek recognized fear. Jurek swallowed and glanced around. Still the gun remained pointed at Tomek's head.

Jurek shook his head. "My orders are not to let anyone in but militia."

In spite of himself, Tomek's heart sent up a prayer. "Jurek, I am going in. Remember who we are, my friend." He touched the rifle head and sensed Jurek stiffen. Gently, he pushed the rifle aside and stepped around Jurek and into the church. He didn't look back.

"Tomek! Thank God!" Professor Lott stood up and waved his arms.

Tomek moved easily through the thinning crowds inside.

Krystyna was holding her ankle with both hands and crying. "It's my fault! I twisted my ankle and can't walk. I told him to leave, Tomek. He does not understand. Or he refuses." She sobbed, her whole body shaking as if in the throes of a fit.

Professor Lott's coat was torn, his face bruised. "I tried to carry her, but I couldn't make it out."

Tomek bent down and picked up Krystyna. "Stay close to me!" he commanded. "Keep your head down."

He went out the way he'd come in. At the entrance, Jurek shuffled, his eyes darting in all directions. Beads of sweat froze on his forehead. Tomek nodded his thanks as he slipped past.

"Move along!" Jurek shouted.

Tomek felt the butt of the rifle come down on his left shoulder. The pain nearly made him drop Krystyna.

Krystyna screamed.

Professor Lott grabbed her and helped support the weight.

It was a clear walk behind the church. In the front churchyard, police vans pulled up. Doors slammed.

"Dad!" Eva came running to them and flung herself at her father.

"Get to the wagon!" Tomek shouted.

Piotrek sat in the driver's seat. "Did you stop for communion, my friend?" he called down.

Tomek hoisted Krystyna to the wagon bed. Eva and her father climbed up and helped get her under the pile of hay. Tomek started to climb up with Piotrek.

"You'd better get under the hay yourself, Tomek!" Piotrek called.

He was right. One farmer would arouse less suspicion. Tomek crawled under the haystack and pulled straw to cover them. His shoulder throbbed with pain.

"I am so sorry." Krystyna had not stopped crying. Her words spilled out between sobs.

"You're fine, Krystyna," Eva said in perfect Polish. "We're all going to be fine."

"*Shhhhh.*" Professor Lott had his arm around Krystyna, calming and quieting her.

The wagon jerked. "*Vi-oooh!*" Piotrek shouted. He turned his horse back up the hill.

Tomek heard boots on concrete coming toward them. He held his breath. The horse trotted, hooves clacking on the pavement. The footsteps veered away, and Tomek let out his breath.

Next to him, Tomek felt Eva's shallow breathing. Then her hand reached across and took his. She held on. Their fingers interlocked. Without speaking, they rode this way, her fingers pressed between his, as the voices and shouts behind them grew fainter.

In the distance, sirens sounded. Somewhere far off a

church bell rang. Through the hay Tomek glimpsed a lone star shining in the black sky. A cloud floated past it, covering it, but the star poked through again.

He should have felt despair, fear, terror. But for the first time in a very long time, in spite of everything, Tomek Muchowiecki felt hope.

⤖ 13 ⤚

Dear Matt,
I can't tell you how much your letter meant to me—

Eva tore off the paper from the yellow tablet, wadded it up, and tossed it into the corner with the others. She tried again.

Hi, Matt,
Thanks for your letter. I'm glad the basketball team beat—

She ripped the page. It tore in the middle. She ripped it again, then threw her pencil into the corner with the failed letter attempts.

Why was it so hard to write Matt? For weeks, all she'd hoped for was a letter from him. And now two had finally been delivered, along with five from Mel, and Eva had no idea what to say to him.

A week had passed since Nowa Huta. Four of her dad's students had been "detained," then released after three days. Janek brought word that they were all okay. But it would be too dangerous for them to return to Zakopane, too risky for everybody. So they'd gone back to their separate schools, where they'd enrolled.

Eva's dad hadn't missed a single class, though. He kept teaching all day long, even when only three of the students showed up in the basement. More than ever, he believed he was needed in Poland. There hadn't been one word about the Nowa Huta arrests in the official Polish news media, not even a write-up on the funeral.

Eva had started sitting in on some of the classes. She knew her father had his students writing actual news accounts and feature articles on what really had taken place in Nowa Huta. Every day, Anna complained that they still didn't have the underground printing press Father B. had promised them when he'd recruited the Zakopane group. But Eva suspected some of the articles they wrote still found their way to the underground press, maybe hand-delivered by Janek.

She shoved Samson off of Matt's letter, unfolded it, and reread the last paragraph. It was the only one that mattered in the page-and-a-half letter. Most of Matt's ramblings seemed to come from a different planet, not just a different country—where people thought about swimming and basketball practice and movies. Matt told her all about his C-minus in world history and what a jerk his computer teacher was. He'd given her a play-by-play of seventh-period study hall and the game against Evanston.

But it was the last paragraph that made her remember the Matt she'd had a crush on since junior high. She had watched him fall in and out of relationships with the most popular girls in school. Then their junior year, he'd suddenly noticed she existed. He'd taken her out for pizza after swim practice, and they'd been together ever since.

Eva, I feel like picking up a phone and hearing your voice. Hard to believe people don't have phones there, or that it would be dangerous for you to use a phone even if you could find one. You're really something to stick it out this long over there. I miss you, Babe.

Love, Matt

Love, Matt. Eva stared at the words. Did he? Did she? Did she love Matt? She'd thought so. Even after they'd been dating for weeks, all she'd have to do was to see him in the hall at school—his lanky body, long blond hair, broad shoulders—and she'd stop and stare, afraid to believe he'd actually chosen *her* out of all the girls in high school.

Still, she couldn't think of anything to say to Matt in this letter.

Eva picked up one of Mel's letters and reread Mel's account of the senior faculty.

Trust me, Eva. You are not missing out by teaching yourself this year. Ms. Andrews, my English teacher, could

have been a shih tzu on steroids in another life. And you
remember Mr. Blake, right? He's still licking his lips like a
mutant lizard. But they both signed my petition to save the
trees in Center Square and keep the new mall from going up
there. So I have to make nice in their classes.

Mel confided in Eva about her parents. Eva knew the Robinsons didn't get along. She could remember her own mother and father arguing, but never like Mr. and Mrs. Robinson. And according to Mel, things were getting worse. Melanie had read articles in the *Chicago Tribune* about the Gdańsk riots, no meat in Warsaw, and the high price of gasoline and necessities throughout Poland, so her letters were filled with questions for Eva to answer.

Reading Mel's letters was almost like having her in the room. Eva had answered her immediately, without coming up for air—detailing the pizza with one-eyed fish, troll lady, even Nowa Huta and Tomek, though not everything about Tomek. She'd left out the part about holding hands with him in the hay wagon.

Eva scooted Samson off her lap and pried herself out of bed. She retrieved the wads of paper and dropped them into the tiny wastebasket. One of Pani Kurczak's chief complaints—and she had a long list—was that the Americans created too much trash. Looking at the overflowing wastebasket, Eva had to admit Pani K. had a point.

She glanced around the bedroom and couldn't help but grin. *Her* side didn't look half bad. It was her dad's side that would have flunked a Pani K. inspection. He'd pulled his blanket over his bed, but it wasn't made. And two pair of socks lay scattered on the floor. Amazing.

Eva smoothed out the bed and picked up. As she was shoving the socks back into the wardrobe, she felt something, pulled it out, and held it up to window light. It was a photograph of her mother. Eva remembered when the picture was taken. She'd taken it herself the summer before the cancer.

The Lott family had gone on a picnic to the lake with her mom's friend Laurie and her family. They'd eaten peanut butter and jelly sandwiches and fought off ants. And Eva had snapped the picture the instant her mom had discovered a giant ant on her arm.

Eva couldn't remember much more about the day, except that it was so normal—maybe the last time Eva experienced normal. After her mother died, Eva had tried to get that normal feeling back. She'd yearned to be part of a normal family again. Since she couldn't, she'd tried everything else. She'd thrown herself into swim practice, into parties, and into her boyfriend. Until this minute, Eva hadn't realized that she'd been searching for a way to feel normal. If her dad had tried to point it out, she wouldn't have listened. But Poland had a way of stripping away the makeup and forcing you to see yourself under it.

For the first time, as she studied the photo of her mother, Eva could see herself there, in her mom's face, her eyes maybe. Or her nose? Eva had always thought, always been told, she looked like her father. But she had her mother in her, too. Here was proof.

Footsteps sounded on the stairs—Dad's. Eva had

learned to recognize them. She slid the photo back where she'd found it and stepped away just before the door opened.

Her dad stuck his head in. "Up for a walk?"

Samson hopped off the bed and ran to greet Eva's dad, no longer the enemy. Eva couldn't remember when that had happened, when the old man's-best-friend adage had kicked in. Dad scratched the little dog's ear. "How's my little Sammy Whammy?" he muttered.

"I've already walked Sammy Whammy, who didn't exactly appreciate the cold," Eva said. "But I wouldn't mind another walk if you're up for it."

They bundled up and headed out toward the Centrum. Eva liked the crunch of their boots on the snow-packed street. The cold air made the skin on her face feel tight. Funny Polish music drifted in from someone's scratchy radio.

They passed the empty butcher shop before either of them spoke. Then Eva's dad said, "I'm glad you've been coming to my classes. I haven't really told you, Eva, how glad I am you came along with me to Zakopane."

"You didn't leave me a lot of choice, Dad." But she grinned at him.

"Tomek told me the way you refused to leave me at the Arka." Frost clouds billowed from his lips. "You remind me a lot of your mother."

Eva couldn't remember the last time he'd talked about Mom. And he'd never said she reminded him of her. "Thanks, Dad," she whispered.

"Do you know what today is?" he asked, as if he hadn't heard her.

Eva had to think. "October eleventh. No, the twelfth, right?" It was so easy to lose track.

"The anniversary of the first time I saw your mother."

"Wait a minute." Eva's mom had told her the story of how she and Eva's dad had met at the University of Oklahoma. Mom was a creative-writing major, and Dad, a graduate in journalism, was working on his doctorate in English. They'd had one class together. "I thought you and Mom got married on the same date you met, October fourteenth, your anniversary."

"That's what your mother thought, too." He grinned down at her.

Eva grinned back, sensing that he was on the verge of telling her a secret. Mom had been full of mother-daughter secrets: "Don't tell your father, but we're going to Florida next year for vacation." "Don't tell your dad, but this family switched to decaf a month ago."

Eva couldn't remember a single secret coming from her dad.

"Go on," she begged, elbowing him.

"Well, she didn't notice me until October fourteenth, but *I* saw *her* the morning of October twelfth. She was wearing a red dress, with tiny buttons down the middle, and she had her hair down. She breezed through the hallway. I saw her coming, and . . ."

"Don't stop now, Dad." Eva was so afraid he'd stop, that she'd never hear this story.

"Well, it was all the clichés, Eva. She took my breath away. My heart pounded. It felt like a thunderbolt." He smiled at her, and Eva thought some of the color in his cheeks might be from blushing. "I stopped her. I asked the time, even though I had a watch right there on my wrist. It was the only thing I could think of. And when she told me, and smiled . . . well, I knew."

"You 'knew'?" Eva repeated.

"I spent the next day—it was the only time I ever missed my classes—finding out about the girl in the red dress. I went to the Arts and Science Department and schmoozed the secretary until I got a name and confirmed she wasn't married. Then I found which class she was taking in the building. And I enrolled."

"You didn't! And you never told her?"

"What, and let her think I was chasing her?" He laughed. Then his eyes turned sad. "People used to say your mother was 'slight' because she was thin and lithe. That woman was anything but slight. She had such a presence, her absence is almost unbearable."

Eva felt tears sting her eyes. She'd known he missed her mother . . . but not like this. Eva recalled scenes of her parents laughing together, just watching TV. She missed seeing that, missed them as a couple. It was a whole new sense of loss. How many other ways were there to miss Mom?

She wanted to make it better, wanted to say something to help her dad. Instead, she reached over and took his hand. She could barely feel his fingers through her thick mittens and his leather gloves. But she knew he was there, and this was all she could do.

"*Rocky?*" Dad stopped on the sidewalk.

"What?" Then Eva saw the billboard outside the only cinema in Zakopane. So far, the movies shown there had been Polish or Russian propaganda films, with a few American psycho-killers-on-the-rampage movies tossed in. Tomek had explained that the only American movies allowed behind the Iron Curtain were the ones that showed the USA in the worst possible light.

But here was *Rocky,* a movie Eva had seen once with Mel and once with Matt. She wondered if Tomek had seen it. She was sure her father hadn't.

She read the time board. "Dad, it's starting right now! Come on! We're going."

"But I have the afternoon class, Eva, and——"

"Hey, this is an anniversary," she said, looking him straight in the eyes. "We're going to the movies."

Her dad let himself be pulled inside, where he forked over złotys that Eva calculated (she'd done her homework since Kraków) came to thirty-eight cents apiece. Inside, the small theater looked as if it had been ritzy a hundred years ago. About thirty Poles were crowded together in the back center of the theater, without a single empty seat between them. The rest of the theater was empty.

As Eva led her dad to a front-row center seat, the show began. It was in English with Polish subtitles. Eva enjoyed it even more than the first two times she'd seen it. And her dad laughed in all the right places. The biggest crowd response from the Polish section came when Rocky walked into a cold storage locker to practice punching on rows and rows of hanging beef carcasses. A collective gasp filled the theater, and Eva wondered for the first time how there could be so much meat in America and none here.

"That was one of the best movies I've ever seen," her dad said, as they left the theater and started back to Widokówka.

They walked in front of the PEWEX shop, a dollar store, where foreigners could purchase Polish products with western currency. Eva stopped and gazed in at the crystal vases and dishes. "Mom would have loved this stuff, wouldn't she?"

Her dad put his arm around her. "Eva, I want to thank you for—"

"Dad, look at that!"

There, in the center of the square, stood a bust of Lenin. Someone had painted it bright pink. Eva couldn't help laughing.

Six militia officers milled around the statue, as if guarding it or trying to decide what to do about it. One of them shouted at two boys walking by and pointing. The boys were questioned. They showed their papers, then left.

"We'd better get out of here," Dad whispered, locking arms with Eva and heading toward Widokówka.

They walked fast and arrived out of breath. Janek and Anna were standing outside smoking.

"Did you see it?" Eva asked, laughing. "The statue of Lenin in town? Somebody painted it pink!"

"All right!" Anna exclaimed, grinning at Janek.

"Not as good as blowing it up, but not bad," Janek said.

Eva and her dad had been in their room about half an hour when someone tapped at the door. Dad had dozed off over *Leaves of Grass,* and Eva was doing homework. "Come in!" Eva called.

Her dad sat up and smoothed his hair.

Andrzej slipped in and closed the door behind him. He reminded Eva of beatniks she'd seen in old movies. She wondered if he liked jazz or played the guitar. He'd come to their room several times over the past few days, usually to ask her dad a theological or political question. Eva had translated, as best she could.

Andrzej took off his beret and twisted it in his hands. "I need to talk with your father, Eva," he said in Polish. "You will translate?"

Eva nodded. "Dad, Andrzej needs to talk with you."

Her father sat on the edge of the bed and motioned Andrzej to sit next to him.

Andrzej sat, then popped up as if the bed were on fire. "It was me!" he exclaimed. "I confess. I am the one who did it!"

➤➤ 14 ◄◄

Eva stared at Andrzej as he paced in tiny circles beside the bed. He looked like a little boy caught with his hand in the cookie jar.

"What did he say?" Eva's dad asked.

Eva translated. "Andrzej said he did it."

Her dad glanced at Andrzej, then back at Eva. "Did *what?*"

Eva was pretty sure she knew what, but she turned to Andrzej and started to translate. Suddenly, Andrzej burst out in broken English, "Lenin! Is pink!"

Eva laughed. Then she hugged him, stepped back, and gave him the thumbs-up.

Andrzej's face turned as pink as Lenin's.

"Dad," she explained, "Andrzej's the one who painted the statue pink."

Her dad's expression was unreadable. He stood up and crossed to the window.

"I was foolish!" Andrzej insisted. "If they find out I did it, I could get us all in trouble. And over such a silly thing I did. Tell me what I should do."

After Eva translated, her dad turned and smiled. Then he walked back and put his arm around Andrzej's shoulder.

Eva couldn't tell if her dad approved or not. But she could see how much he cared for Andrzej.

"Andrzej, don't tell anyone about this," he said. He waited for Eva to translate. "The militia we saw in the square didn't look like they had any idea who did it. Let's keep it that way."

Andrzej looked relieved as he shook hands with Eva's father and thanked them both. He put on his beret and left smiling.

Eva watched her dad as he took his *Norton Anthology* out from under the bed and settled in with his notebook. It struck her what a good job he was doing with everything. He couldn't even understand the language, but he had a connection with the students.

She started to go back to her lit book, then changed her mind. Maybe she could find Tomek and see what he thought about the pink Lenin. Since Nowa Huta, she hadn't had one minute alone with him. It felt like he was avoiding her, but she knew she might have been the one doing the avoiding.

"I'll be back in a while," she told her dad, as she pulled on her shoes. She slipped into a clean sweater and headed out the door, making as little racket as possible, so Samson wouldn't want to come.

The door swung open and rammed into Grażyna. Grażyna stumbled backward, bumping into her mop bucket. Murky water splashed everywhere.

Eva got down on hands and knees to help mop up the mess. "I'm so sorry, Grażyna!" She glanced at the older girl, whose red hair was tied back in a triangular scarf, making her look the part of a scrub woman. Eva felt even worse for adding to her work.

Eva hated housework of any kind. Since Nowa Huta and the loss of Tymoteusz, Marek, and the others, Eva had been forced to help out more in the day-to-day running of Widokówka. They'd all doubled up on chores, but it seemed Grażyna got the worst of it.

"You're sure I didn't hurt you?" Eva asked, trying to peer into the tired eyes of the other girl.

"I am fine," Grażyna insisted. "Are you okay, Eva?" Grażyna asked it in English, surprising Eva. She had never heard Grażyna speak English before.

"Your English is good!" Eva exclaimed.

Grażyna shrugged. "Not so good. But thank you for saying it." They were back in Polish now. "Poor Eva."

Eva was confused. Grażyna was the one Eva felt sorry for. She couldn't be happy missing out on everything, mopping and cleaning every day for the others. "Poor Eva?"

"You miss friends," Grażyna explained. "Eva has other American friends in Poland? Others like your papa in other Poland cities?"

"Nope. We don't know any other Americans here."

Eva studied Grażyna. She'd probably be pretty if she wore her hair down and used a little makeup and maybe did something besides scrubbing floors all day for Father B.

"Your father goes to Warsaw," Grażyna said. "You have no friends there?"

Eva shook her head. As far as she knew, her dad had only made one trip to Warsaw, about a month ago. He hadn't taken her . . . maybe because she'd been throwing a tantrum at the time, refusing to leave the room until he agreed to send her back to America.

"Grażyna," Eva said, "you should come to Dad's classes. I know you eavesdrop on them. *I* did the same thing before I decided to attend. Why don't you take the classes, like Anna does?"

"I am not so smart as Anna and Tomek." She stared at her mop bucket. "It is okay. I am content to help. I do what I can do. It is enough."

Eva didn't know what else to say. She helped finish mopping up the spill. Then she searched the house for Tomek. But he wasn't there.

Tomek didn't show up for supper, either. Eva tried not to think about him or imagine where he was, what he was doing. But during the night, every time she heard footsteps on the stairs, she ran to the door and peeked out, hoping to see Tomek.

The next day, Eva's dad woke her with the most hated words in the entire English language: "Kitchen duty!"

Groaning, she grabbed Samson and pulled the covers over both of them. Eva would rather sweep ten houses than wash one more dish.

It was still dark outside, but the house stirred as if it were high noon. It was positively un-American to be up so early.

Her dad yanked off the covers. "They're shorthanded."

"No kidding," she mumbled, pulling the pillow over her head. Eva had washed more dishes in the past week than she had in her entire past. Her hands looked like her grandmother's. Since southern Poles couldn't get soap this time of year, they killed bacteria by washing dishes in boiling water.

"Sooner you start, the sooner you'll finish." In spite of his deep voice, her father could sound horribly cheery in the morning.

Eva groaned and rolled out of bed. Samson burrowed back under the blanket, giving new meaning to *lucky dog*.

Halfway down the stairs, Eva heard Tomek's voice floating up from the basement. She ran her fingers through her hair and hurried down. When she walked into the kitchen, Tomek and Anna were laughing. They leaned against the counter, sipping coffee together, holding their small glasses by the rim in exactly the same way.

Eva tried not to look away. Anna was one of the most beautiful girls—women—she'd ever seen off the movie screen. Her fierce green eyes were locked on Tomek, who seemed to lap up every word she was saying.

"*Dzień dobry*, Eva!" Grażyna called from the stove. She was shoving in cardboard and coal for her fire.

"*Dzień dobry*, Grażyna," Eva answered.

Anna turned to Eva and raised her eyebrows as if surprised to see her show up for work. Then she picked up a stack of plates from the counter and held them out to Eva. "Tell her to set the table," she said to Tomek in Polish.

Since Nowa Huta, Eva had been speaking in Polish to everyone in the house, even Pani K. She hadn't needed Tomek to interpret for her, which was a good thing, since he hadn't been around. And now, Eva suspected she knew why. Anna. Well, fine. She didn't need him, anyway.

Eva took the plates from Anna, repressing the urge to throw them at her.

"Anna wants you—," Tomek actually started to translate for her.

Eva stopped him with her best Polish. "Why, I'd be thrilled to set these plates on that table. Wouldn't want your coffees to get cold." She could have said plenty more. Plenty. Tomek had been acting weird ever since they'd left Piotrek's wagon.

Krystyna hobbled in, her ankle bound in bandages with an odd, homemade casting on top that cracked and shed brown flakes wherever she hopped. She'd refused to go to a doctor after Nowa Huta, but a neighbor had been brought in. Eva's dad called her a midwife.

"Dzień dobry!" Krystyna called.

"Is the ankle any better?" Eva asked, making Krystyna lean on her to get to the bench. Eva admired her for never complaining about her ankle, even though her foot was still too swollen for slippers.

Krystyna smiled, and her tiny eyes disappeared above chubby cheeks. "It's fine! Let me help you with the table." She started to get up.

"Nie!" Eva made her sit while she finished setting out the plates herself. She set down a glass in front of

Krystyna and noticed a letter in her friend's lap. "Mail?" she teased. "Krystyna has a secret admirer!"

Krystyna looked puzzled, then laughed. "I must have twisted my head as well as my ankle." She turned to Tomek. "Tomek, this letter just came for you."

Grażyna joined Krystyna and tapped Tomek's letter. "You should let me get the post for you, Krystyna," she said. "I will go and see if there is more." She walked out of the kitchen and up the steps.

Tomek set down his glass of coffee—Eva still hadn't gotten used to the fact that Poles actually preferred their hot drinks in clear glasses instead of mugs—and crossed the room for his letter. He opened the thin envelope and took out a single sheet.

Eva watched his eyes as he read. They flickered with anger or fear. He bit on his bottom lip and ran one hand over his hair. Without looking up, he folded the letter, put it back into the envelope, and slipped it into his pocket.

"What is it?" Eva asked.

He turned and looked into her eyes, his gaze making it hard for her to breathe. For a minute he didn't speak, and neither did she.

"I must go." He said it in Polish. Then he said it louder, to the whole room. "I must go. Tell Father B. and Professor Lott."

"Tomek?" Eva followed him. He walked toward the sink, turned, and paced back. "Where? Where are you going?"

"To Brzegi," he answered. "My father needs me. I must go home to pick a plum."

He was mumbling, but she thought that's what he'd said. She wasn't sure about the word for *plum*, though. He paced to the window.

Eva whispered to Krystyna, "Did he say 'pick a plum'? Like the little hard fruit with the rough pit thing inside?"

Krystyna nodded. "Tomek's father owns a plum or-chard. I think there is ice storm on the way. Maybe he goes to help harvest."

"How can you know there's an ice storm coming?" The only television she'd seen had been in the window of a shop in Kraków. And the show playing was a rerun of *Kojak*, the bald American detective. She'd only heard one scratchy radio, and that was outside Widokówka.

"The rings around the moon last night, Eva. Did you not see them?" Krystyna winced and lifted her bad ankle onto the bench with both hands. "That means rain in two days, or an ice storm on the way. Tomek's father must get in his crop."

Anna plopped a handful of silverware into Eva's palm and pointed at the table. Then *she* went over to Tomek and put her arm around him. They whispered together as Eva plunked down forks and spoons as loudly as she could.

Eva didn't buy into this rings-around-the-moon the-ory. It sounded too much like the time Krystyna was so afraid for Eva's father because a spider had crawled across his wallet.

Anna still had her arm around Tomek. He was milk-ing this for all it was worth. He'd probably take off to his home and leave them even more shorthanded than they were already. Anna wouldn't be the one to get extra duties, either. Eva would. It wasn't fair.

Eva set down the rest of the forks. An idea was forming in the back of her mind. For days she'd been little more than a galley slave. Maybe it was time to get herself out of the kitchen. Anything had to be better than washing another dish in boiling water.

Anna took out bread and made sandwiches, while Tomek looked on. Eva strolled over to them.

"Tomek?" Eva put her hand on his shoulder the way Anna had done. "Listen. Let me come with you. I could help pick your father's plums. Wouldn't another person be good?"

Anna made a harsh animal noise. She wrapped a sandwich in brown paper. "I do not think it is good. Pani Kurczak must need Eva."

"Get serious! Pani K. can't stand me in her kitchen. She'll be glad to get rid of me for a day." Eva was answering Anna's Polish with Polish, and Anna wasn't pretending she couldn't understand. It wasn't Anna's business, anyway. If Eva wanted to help Tomek, then that was between Tomek and her. And Dad . . . And maybe Anna was right about Pani K. The woman was a force.

"So you think Pani Kurczak will be fine to have you miss kitchen duty, Eva?" Anna asked.

"Absolutely."

"Why don't you ask her, then?" Anna's smile was mean. She pointed behind Eva to where Pani K. had just walked in with Eva's dad.

Pani K.'s eyes narrowed, making her nose look even

sharper. Her dyed brown hair was pulled into a tiny pony-tail, and she wore a pink velvet pantsuit. "I can't lose one more person in this house or we will not produce meals!"

Looking smug, Anna turned back to the sink.

"What's going on, Eva? What are they saying?" Eva's dad had his arms full of books, plus Pani K.'s shopping bag.

"Dad, Tomek's family needs me to help them bring in their plums before the ice storm. Is it okay if I go home with him? He lives in Brzegi, that little village the bus goes by. Please?" For once she was glad her dad and Anna couldn't understand each other. Anna would be right there to tell him a whole different version of this story.

Her dad squeezed the bridge of his nose. "What will I do with the class while Tomek's gone?"

Good. He was more worried about Tomek leaving than her. "Have them read . . . and write, Dad. It's just one day. Besides, this isn't about you or the class. It's about Tomek's father and his orchard." She felt a twinge of guilt, knowing that, for her, this was more about kitchen duty than orchard rescuing. Rings around the moon? She and Tomek would probably get to Brzegi only to discover the plums were just fine. But at the very least she could miss an entire day of dishes.

"You're right, Eva. Of course." Her father always had been a sucker for guilt. "You should go."

"Yes!"

Pani K. hadn't stopped scowling. "I don't know what they are saying," she barked. "We have not enough people in the kitchen right now."

Krystyna came to the rescue, explaining about the threat to the orchard and promising she was well enough to help in the kitchen again.

Finally, Pani K. agreed. "I saw this ring around the moon," she said, shaking her finger at Eva, as if warning her. "You go. You help. You come back. There will be plenty of work in this kitchen when you return."

Even Pani Kurczak's parting shot couldn't ruin this. Eva was getting out of kitchen duty! She just hoped Anna would have to take up the slack.

↦ 15 ↤

It was still dark as Eva threw some things together and kissed her dad and Samson good-bye.

Tomek was waiting at the door, and they stepped outside into air so cold it froze her breath. The ground crackled under their boots as if they were walking on broken glass. They climbed the hill to the bus stop, with stars and moon still shedding more light than the rising sun. In the fields along the path, little mounds of hay cast eerie shadows, like slumped, chubby soldiers in a row.

At the bus stop Eva shifted her weight from foot to foot so her toes wouldn't freeze.

Tomek stood still as the North Star. Finally he spoke to her . . . in English. "My parents will like to meet you."

Eva grinned. She hadn't been sure if Tomek wanted her along or not. Still, the thought of meeting his parents unnerved her. What if they didn't like her? What if Tomek had already told them she was a spoiled American?

When the bus pulled in, almost forty minutes late, Eva hopped on and headed for the back. But Tomek touched her arm to stop her and nodded at a seat toward the front. "Back is big bumps," he whispered.

Tomek knew what he was talking about. Even in the front Eva bounced so hard she left the bus seat and once bumped her head on the roof, though Tomek didn't seem to notice.

They passed through a village with nothing but four thatch-roofed cottages. A woman got on with a chicken under each arm and sat in the back. The chickens squawked and *puck-pucked,* and Eva found herself rooting for them to make a run for it.

The old woman greeted each new passenger as if they were relatives. In fact, everyone on the bus, even Tomek, greeted passengers with handshakes or *"Dzień dobry."*

Eva had just resigned herself to thinking that, for whatever reason, Tomek had decided she wasn't worth talking to anymore, when he said her name. "Eva?" He stared ahead, not glancing at her. "Where's your mother?"

The question took her completely by surprise, like a snowball broadsiding her. Her first week in Poland, she'd expected people to ask. When they didn't, she'd assumed everybody knew her mother was dead. Surely Tomek had to know that.

"She died." She stared out the window at the way the sun was turning the countryside orange and yellow and red. In a field, two horses struggled in front of a plow. She wondered if Tomek understood the word *cancer.*

She could have stopped there. Tomek wouldn't have

pried. They could have finished the trip in total silence. But for some reason she went on.

Eva sat back in the seat and glanced at Tomek to see if he was even listening.

He nodded for her to go on.

"After Mom got sick, I used to stay late at school on purpose," Eva admitted. It was a secret she'd never even told Melanie. "I didn't want to see how she'd changed. I wanted to think of her like she had been before."

Eva thought of everything in terms of before and after Mom. She remembered every detail of the last *before* moment. Eva had just wriggled out of her wet swimsuit and into her green terrycloth robe. She'd been brushing her hair, watching herself in the dresser mirror. Tiny drops of water stuck to the mirror as she flipped her wet hair over her shoulder. Eva had seen her dad's reflection first. The radio was playing "One of These Nights," by the Eagles, a song Mel had told her about but she'd never heard before. The air was tinged with chlorine from her wet suit.

She'd stopped brushing. Before she even turned around to see her dad's tears and listen to his broken words about Mom, about cancer, she'd known. The world had split in two—before and after.

"After Mom got cancer, I hoped it would go away. I prayed it would go away. It didn't." Eva had never told her dad this—not then, and not after.

"Then I hoped at least it wouldn't hurt her so much, that she wouldn't suffer from it." Eva felt her throat heat up with warm tears. She swallowed them and made herself go on. "But it got worse. And the treatments left her so weak. You could smell the pain. I know that sounds crazy, but you could."

Tomek put his hand on hers and left it there.

"One night I heard the doctor tell Dad that it could go to Mom's brain. I hoped so hard it wouldn't. When it did, there wasn't anything left to hope for. I stopped hoping."

They rode quietly for a while. Hills rolled by outside the bus window. Farmers behind horse-drawn wagons loaded hay from fields that looked like patchwork quilts. Then Tomek pulled out his brown bag of sandwiches and handed one to Eva. "For you. Lard."

Her stomach did a flashback and threatened a rebellion. She unwrapped the sandwich. Cheese and bread. Eva burst out laughing. A joke? From Tomek?

All over the bus, as if on cue, passengers pulled out bread or kielbasa or cheese and joined in a silent communal meal.

Eva ate, then dozed off to dreams of her mother cheering her on at a swim meet. Mom's voice grew deeper and louder, then turned into Tomek's.

"*Prędzej, prędzej!*" Tomek stood up. The bus had stopped.

Still in a daze, she stumbled after him, while voices on the bus called good-bye in Polish and deeply accented English.

The driver shouted, "I have uncle in Chicago!" And everybody laughed.

"How did he know I'm from Chicago?" Eva asked, nodding to the man.

Tomek grinned. "He doesn't. Everybody in Poland has an uncle in Chicago."

Eva waved as the bus pulled away in a black cough of gritty smoke, leaving them in the middle of nowhere.

Tomek stood and surveyed the fields and the road.

"Were you expecting somebody to be here?" Eva asked.

He shook his head. "But even here in the country, there may be watchers." He peered up the lane one more time, then dashed across the dirt road and down the hill.

Eva ran after him, through pine trees and bushes. The cool wind numbed her cheeks, but the sunshine made her squint. They got the storm prediction wrong, she thought. And Tomek's paranoid. Nothing and no one could be in danger on a day like this.

At last she saw, in the distance, smoke rising from a chimney. Tomek picked up the pace. Ahead lay a small shed and what looked like a larger shack or cabin. Beside it, a line of laundry waved stiffly in the wind. A tall wooden cross rested against the shingled side of the house, as if tossed there, like a pogo stick. From the step in front of the shack, someone was waving wildly.

"Papa!" Tomek shouted, running into the arms of his father.

A short stocky woman, her head covered with a paisley triangular scarf, stepped outside and joined in the hug. At her feet a small boy clung to her dress.

Tomek motioned for Eva to join them. "This is my friend from America, Eva Lott." He spoke Polish now.

"Her father is our professor in Zakopane. Eva has come to help with the harvest."

To Eva he said in English, "My mother speaks no English. My father, yes, good English. Stash, a little. This is Stash, my little cousin." Tomek roughed up the boy's bushy hair, black as his own.

None of Eva's friends could speak two languages, not even Korbie, and she was actually Korean.

"Thanks . . . you . . . helping!" bellowed Tomek's father, a short dark-haired version of Santa Claus. He looked as if at any minute he might break out into *ho, ho, ho*. "We are proud to have girl from America in our home!"

Eva stuck out her hand to shake, but Tomek's parents hugged her instead and pulled her inside. The house was as close to a log cabin as Eva had ever been in. The only picture on the wall had been torn from a magazine, a portrait of the Pope who had died shortly after Eva and her dad had arrived in Poland. It had been a day of mourning for the entire country. People had called the Pope "Papa" and grieved as if he had actually been a family member.

Eva tried to imagine how the whole family could live in such a small space. She'd half hoped she'd end up spending the night so she could miss another day of kitchen duty. Now she could see there wouldn't be any place to sleep overnight.

Pani Muchowiecka brought out *herbatka* (hot tea) and sweet breads, which Tomek and Eva downed while his parents watched and Stash peeked from his spot in the corner.

"*Smacznego!*" Tomek's dad declared, holding out the plate of breads to Eva.

She'd already had two pieces. The breads didn't taste sweet, but they weren't bad. She ate one more and started to carry her dish to the sink, but Tomek's mother took it from her.

"Shouldn't we start picking?" Eva asked, working hard to use good Polish grammar. It wasn't easy. Even the verbs had male and female forms.

"*Tak!*" Papa Muchowiecki shouted, pounding the table as if Eva had just come up with a startling idea. "This is good! Eva says pick. We pick!"

Tomek and his father walked arm in arm to the orchard, talking too low for Eva to make out what they were saying, but she heard "militia" and "problem." She struggled to keep up, picking her way through the rutted pasture and down a rocky hillside.

Somewhere behind her an engine roared. Her first thought was *tanks*. She turned in time to see a battered truck bounce over the hill. Four men stood in the back of the truck, whooping and laughing. They sped past her and jerked to a dusty stop. The men hopped out, each carrying a wooden crate. Little Stash climbed out after them.

"These are cousins," Tomek explained. "And neighbors come to help."

They looked wild and windblown, like Polish cowboys. Eva couldn't guess their ages, whether they were men or boys. Each one removed his hat and shook hands with Tomek, with his father, and then with Eva.

The tallest man waited until last, frowning at Eva as he gave her hand one firm shake. "*Amerykanka?*" he asked, shaking his head in disapproval. He spit on the ground, but Eva didn't know if it had anything to do with the fact that she was American. His Adam's apple stuck out like a second chin. His hair was lighter than the others', coarse like straw. He didn't look a bit like Tomek.

"That's Łukasz," Stash whispered. "Don't mind him."

The man looked brittle, his face tan and leathery.

The cousins elbowed each other, then raced up the next hill and out of sight. Eva followed at a brisk walk, wondering where they kept the plums. So far she hadn't seen a single one, just a pasture that hadn't been mowed for a long time and was too rocky to grow the crops she knew about.

At the top of the next hill, she got her first glimpse of the orchard. Low, tangled trees blanketed the deep valley. Black branches curved and interlocked, like ancient fingers praying. Purple plums dotted the rows of trees like colorful Christmas ornaments. Eva hadn't expected it to be beautiful.

"You take this row." Tomek pointed to the nearest line of trees. "Stash will help you."

"I don't want to babysit," Eva protested. "I really do want to help pick."

Tomek looked confused as he hoisted a wooden crate under one arm as if it were a football. "I do not understand sit baby? Stash is a good worker. He will help." He rolled up the sleeves of his plaid flannel shirt and headed out into the orchard. After a few steps, he called back over his shoulder, "Pick only ripe plums!"

"No, Tomek." His father, standing a few feet from Eva, hadn't raised his voice, but even Łukasz and the cousins stopped their joking and turned to him. The orchard grew still except for the caw of a bird in the distance.

"You must pick all plums," he said in Polish, moving his gaze from one to the other.

Tomek stiffened. "All?" His eyes widened as he stared at his father. "Pick all?"

"Pick all plums today," he answered. "From every tree. For we may not have tomorrow."

➼ 16 ⤛

Without a word, Tomek dropped his crate at the base of a tree and began picking Eva's row. He seemed more frightened than he had at Nowa Huta, as if ice might pose a greater threat than tanks.

Eva took one of the crates and carried it to the other side of the row. She pulled her first plum off a low branch. Next to her, Stash already had four plums in the box they shared. He moved fast and soundlessly. But after a few minutes, even with two of them, they lagged behind Tomek.

Time passed and the others walked by with loaded crates to empty into the truck. Łukasz peered into Eva's half-empty box and shook his head.

Eva determined to get faster. She watched the way Stash's hands worked together. She'd only been picking right-handed. Now she forced her left hand to pick, too.

Although she dropped plums at first, gradually she got better, matching Stash almost plum for plum.

"Yes! Good, Eva!" Papa Muchowiecki called as he carried yet another crate to the truck. He broke into a Polish folk song Krystyna had tried to teach Eva at Widokówka. One by one the others joined in with off-key singing that could scare crows.

The neighbor man, who looked like a fugitive from a circus, maybe a lion-tamer, started the next song. Eva knew it, "Amazing Grace." While they sang in Polish, she sang in English, remembering a rainy morning when she'd stood next to her mother in church, singing that same song. She'd mouthed the words then so she could listen to her mom's clear voice, the way she seemed to be transported by the words, amazed by the promise of grace.

The plunking of plums into crates, the shuffling of feet on sticks, the cawing of crows deep in the pasture made a kind of background music. The more Eva sang, the more nimble her fingers became. Her left hand cooperated. She picked up speed. They sang song after song, Eva chiming in with a mixture of English, Polish, and gibberish when she didn't know the tune.

Before long, she was staying ahead of Stash, and they reached the end of their second row. She and Stash carried their box to the truck and handed it up to a neighbor.

"Bravo!" The cousin named Arek clapped as he waited with his crate.

The older neighbor, standing in the pickup bed, emptied Eva's crate, then joined in the applause. So did two of the cousins behind her.

Eva smiled and took a bow. The crate was handed down from the truck. She grabbed it and turned around, almost crashing into Tomek and his overflowing crate of plums. He didn't crack a smile.

"*Przepraszam,*" Eva said. "*Wiem, że to trudne.*" Sorry. *I know it's difficult.*

Tomek's cousin Łukasz let out a harsh laugh as he pushed past her to hand up his box. He glared at her, his lips a disapproving line.

Tomek didn't stand up for her. He just stepped in front of her to hand Arek his crate.

Eva felt her face flush. They had no right to treat her like a spoiled child or an idiot. "Come on, Stash," she whispered. "We'll show them."

Stash grinned up at her. They were in this together now. She led him to the section of orchard where Łukasz and Tomek were picking and plopped down their crate directly opposite the pair, on the other side of the row. Through the black branch canopy, Eva watched Łukasz's hands reaching high and low as his feet shuffled steadily down the row of plums.

Eva cracked her knuckles and settled down to business, leaving Tomek to Stash. She kept herself in motion, each hand plucking those plums as if the weight of the whole orchard rested on her alone. Stash followed behind her, climbing into a tree for the highest branches, but she kept moving farther and farther down the row.

On the other side, Łukasz stayed ahead of her, but not by much. She kept sight of his brown sweater and corduroy pants through the branches as she forced herself to go faster. Twice she caught Łukasz glancing back at her, pretending not to. Working harder, she pushed herself until she couldn't feel her fingers as they picked and dropped, picked and dropped, the sound turning into a primitive music all its own.

Gradually she became aware of a murmur behind her. Without slowing down, she peeked over her shoulder. Tomek and his dad stood together, watching. She glimpsed Stash staring down from a high branch. The neighbor and cousins lined the field behind her, watching, not picking.

Eva pushed herself harder, faster. Her hands ached. Her feet hurt. Still, she picked and picked, pushing the box ahead with her foot as she moved down the row, stretching her leg to cover more ground.

"Go, Eva!" Stash shouted.

The others cheered, "Eva! Eva!," shouting her name over and over.

Almost to the end now, she glanced through the branches and found herself face to face with an astonished Łukasz. He stopped picking and stared at her with eyes wide as plums. His boot kicked at his crate, shoving it too hard. The crate slid, then overturned. Purple plums rolled at his feet. Łukasz had to scramble on hands and knees to retrieve them.

The spectators jeered, laughing so hard Eva couldn't make out what they were saying.

She focused. She couldn't slow down now. Not now. The end of her row came into sight, a patch of white at the end of shade.

Behind her Łukasz was back on track now, coming up

fast. Eva heard the rapid *pluck, pluck, drop,* the scrape of his crate on the ground. He was so fast.

She heard Tomek's dad laugh as the cheers grew louder.

One more branch. She saw Łukasz on the other side. *Pluck-drop* . . . And she finished!

A half second later Łukasz plopped his full crate next to hers. Hoots and whistles exploded around her.

Eva leaned over to catch her breath. She had never felt so completely drained, yet almost electrified. When she stood up, Łukasz held out his hand to shake. He nodded with a trace of a smile. They shook hands, and the crowd broke loose again with congratulations and pats on the back that nearly knocked her over. Tomek's dad lifted her off the ground in an embrace. When he let her down, she looked around for Tomek.

He was carrying his crate to the next row of trees.

Silently they all took their crates back into the orchard.

The sun had moved past its peak when Tomek's mother walked out to the orchards. Watching her come through the fields, her skirts held up in one fist, a black pouch in the other, Eva could imagine that they had moved back in time a century. Two other women in long dresses, their heads covered with kerchief scarves, slogged through the brush, carrying baskets. One of the women spread out a blanket next to the truck, and the others unloaded their bags.

"*Obiad!*" Pani Muchowiecka shouted.

Eva's back had ached for the last hour, but she didn't want to stop. She wanted to finish her row. She kept picking as others walked past her.

"Eva, come!" ordered Papa Muchowiecki. "When Mama says to come, we come!"

Eva left her crate and joined the others. They ate cheese and bread and something that might have been sausage. Back at Widokówka, she was always the one who tried to drag out meals and put off dishes as long as possible. But now, as soon as she'd finished her bread, she jogged back to the orchard with Stash.

All afternoon they picked. Darkness crept in unnoticed until the plums all looked the same color under the setting sun. With the darkness came a deep, cutting chill and a breeze from the north. Eva didn't know if her hands were stiff from the labor or from the cold wind that reached inside her coat and under her gloves. Every muscle ached, but her fingers kept picking as if on automatic.

A bell sounded from the house. Tomek's dad picked up his crate and bellowed, "That is it! We will stop! Come! Basia waits supper. She will be in fury!"

Eva didn't object. She fell in with Stash, Tomek, and the others. "We didn't get to half of the trees," Eva whispered.

"Maybe the ice will wait another day," Stash whispered back.

Tomek didn't answer. He seemed to be a thousand miles away as they crossed the field and came up behind the house.

Again Eva noticed the splintered cross, looking out of place next to a hoe and what looked like a walking stick. "What's with the cross?" she asked Stash.

She saw him glance over at Tomek. Then he sucked his lips in and shook his head. "You should ask Tomek."

She wouldn't. Not now, when he'd moved as far away from her as if he were back in Zakopane.

As soon as Eva felt the warmth of the house fire, she realized how sore she really was. Her legs shook with weakness, and she couldn't feel her fingers or toes. Tomek's mother, who acted shy around Eva, not looking at her or speaking directly to her, poured water on Eva's and Stash's hands. It stung like a million pinpricks.

The whole crew took their places at the too-small table, and Tomek's father said grace. Eva caught most of it—thanksgiving and requests to the "Lord of the Harvest." She peeked and caught Stash peeking at her. They exchanged guilty grins and looked back at their plates.

Tomek's mother put two of what looked like dumplings on Eva's plate first, then two on the other plates around the table.

"Pierogi," Stash whispered to her, with an air of Christmas Eve excitement. "You will like."

"I'm so hungry, I'd eat lard," Eva whispered back.

In record time she devoured bigos, pierogi with meat and sauerkraut inside, soup, and bread. Never had food tasted so wonderful. It was a noisy meal, punctuated with loud laughter and mock arguments.

When the cousins finally went home, the white linen—

covered table was turned back into a rough wooden worktable. Tomek offered to help his mother make plum pierogi for the next day.

"I'd like to help, too," Eva said, "if you'll show me how, Pani Muchowiecka."

The woman smiled without showing her teeth and nodded. She took off her own apron and tied it around Eva, wrapping the apron strings twice around.

A dim lightbulb hung over the table. The cord swung back and forth, casting moving shadows around the kitchen. Tomek's mother stood over her sink, mixing dough for them. It made Eva think of her own mother making dough for Christmas cutout cookies.

As they rolled dough into a thin paper, Papa told stories. He talked about his grandfather, who had taught in the underground, in "Flying Universities" in Warsaw before World War One. At first Eva had to stop and ask Tomek the meaning of certain Polish words. But after a while, she discovered she could understand the stories on her own, her mind filling in for the Polish words she didn't know. It was like reading a book that was hard, with big words that could still be understood in context.

"When I was a young boy," Papa began, his fists pushing into a bowl of dough, "Hitler marched through Europe and took our country. Many Poles, like my father and Father Blachnicki, refused the Germans and fought in the Polish Underground resistance. Both my father and Father B. were arrested and sent to Auschwitz concentration camp."

Eva had studied the Holocaust in her world history

class. She remembered the pictures of the barbed-wire death camps, the skeletons in striped clothing, walking and being carried out of Auschwitz. But the prisoners were all Jewish. "I . . . I don't understand." She glanced at Tomek's father. The bulb overhead threw a strip of light on his leathery face. "Why would the Nazis arrest *them*? They weren't Jewish."

He smiled at her as he would have at a little girl. "The Jews suffered total destruction in Poland, but they were not alone. Our German captors had more cruelty in them. Eleven million people were killed during the Holocaust. Six million were Polish citizens—half Polish Jews, half Polish Christians. Heinrich Himmler, the head of the Nazi police forces, issued a proclamation: 'All Poles will disappear from the world . . . It is essential that the great German people should consider it as its major task to destroy all Poles.'"

For a few minutes there was no sound except the rushing of wind outside and the gentle *shush, shush, shush* of the dough beneath the roller.

"What happened to your father?" Eva asked.

"He died in Auschwitz. Blachnicki was taken, along with thousands of Catholic priests and Christian pastors, to Dachau, a concentration camp near Munich, Germany, a special barracks where religious men were executed or left to die of starvation and disease. But Father B. survived to fight the next oppressor."

From time to time Eva glanced at Tomek. He kept his eyes cast down as he worked with his own bowl of dough. When he finally spoke, his hands kept punching the dough, hard, with closed fists. "And so, I never knew my grandfather."

Tomek's father sighed and wiped his forehead with his arm. His wife reached around and brushed a shock of black-gray hair away from his face. "You would have liked him so, Tomek," Papa said. "Your grandfather looked much like your brother."

"Tomek has a brother?" Eva asked. She turned to Tomek. "Why didn't you tell me? Where is he?"

Tomek slowly looked up at her, swallowed, then said, "Tadeusz is dead."

Eva's chest burned. Part of her wished she hadn't asked the question. Part of her wanted to ask a hundred more. But Tomek wouldn't look at her again.

Papa expertly slid the pit from a plum, wrapped dough around the purple skin, then pinched it shut. "Tadeusz hoped for a free, independent Poland. When he was barely seventeen, he moved to Gdańsk to work in the Lenin Shipyard. He wanted to help people like Anna Walentynowicz and Lech Wałęsa in this struggle for freedom."

There were words she couldn't make out, but she understood enough. Eva tried to fold her plum in the dough and pinch it shut, but it wouldn't stay. She wanted him to keep talking, to tell her everything about Tomek's brother. Maybe, somehow, it would explain Tomek's anger, the sadness she'd seen in him.

Tomek's dad glanced at his wife, as if asking permission before going on. "In December of 1970, the government hiked food prices and fired many workers. So the workers went on strike, which our government called riots."

But it was Tomek who put an end to the story. "The militia showed up in tanks and with rifles and machine guns to shoot into the crowd. Tadeusz was gunned down in the massacre. And I lost my brother." He didn't look up as he talked, but kept folding dough around plums, faster and faster.

"He did not have a chance." Papa Muchowiecki spat out the words. "He could not run with his bad leg. He died in the street."

Tomek's mother hadn't said anything as she washed the plums and set them on the table, taking the finished ones to a pan on the counter. Now she set down plums on the table but didn't release them. "And they were the ones who gave him this bad leg," she said softly.

Eva thought she had never seen eyes so filled with controlled sorrow.

While his wife returned to the sink, Papa explained. "You have maybe seen the cross we still have, Eva?"

She nodded, remembering the old cross she'd noticed leaning against the house.

"Tadeusz and his cousins, like many other teens in Poland, then as now, enjoyed doing what they could to defy the militia. They climbed to the high hills and planted crosses, a thing forbidden by our atheist government. Most of the crosses remained there because our fat militia officers were too lazy and out of shape to climb up and take them down."

"And people still do it now?" Eva asked, placing two plums she'd covered with dough onto the pan.

"They do." Papa passed the tray filled with dough-covered plums to his wife. "Do they not, Tomek?"

Tomek grinned as he wrapped a small purple plum with his big fingers. "Oasis plants crosses everywhere. Andrzej is the best."

Eva thought of Andrzej's confession to her father that he had painted the Lenin statue pink. "I really like Andrzej," she said.

Papa turned and winked at his wife, who was drying another pan. "She would have liked Tadeusz, eh, Basia?" He turned back in his chair and dipped his hands in for more dough. "But Tadeusz and the boys were not so lucky once. They climbed the highest peak of the Tatras, above Morskie Oko, not so far from Zakopane. And when they came down, two militia waited. When the boys refused to go up and take the crosses down, the soldiers arrested Tadeusz and his friend Zbyszek, though Łukasz escaped."

As if he couldn't take it any longer, Tomek got up and walked out of the room.

"Tadeusz would never speak of this arrest or tell us what happened at the police station," Papa continued, his voice low. "But his friend lost an eye, and my son's knee was destroyed. From that point, he could never again walk, only dragging his leg alongside."

Tears burned in her throat. "I'm so sorry . . . ." Nothing she could think of to say was enough. "But Łukasz? They didn't hurt him?"

"Łukasz was hurt for life, only where you cannot see it." Papa was quiet for a minute before adding, "When Łukasz came home, he had the cross with him and gave it to Tadeusz's mother. We never speak of this day."

Eva was honored that they'd shared so much of themselves with her. She ached for Tomek. She wanted to hold him, to comfort him. But she knew he wouldn't let her.

⇥ 17 ⇤

By the time they had turned the kitchen/living room into a bedroom for the night, Eva could have slept standing up. She kept her coat on over long underwear and a wool nightgown. Pani Muchowiecka gave Eva a pillow and blanket for the folded-down couch, which had probably been Tomek's. Tonight he sat on the picnic blanket in the corner of the room, reading with the only light in the house.

Eva turned her face to the wall and shut her eyes, but sleep didn't come. She'd heard about people being too tired to sleep, but she hadn't believed it until now. Finally, she gave up and rolled over. Tomek was still reading.

"Tomek, I can't sleep. Read to me." She expected him to ignore her or tell her to leave him alone.

Instead, he got up, walked to the kitchen, and returned with a lit kerosene lantern. Tomek sat on the floor, his back resting against her couch, while the light spilled gold onto both of them. Without explanation, he read to her poems of Czesław Miłosz, first in Polish, then translating into English.

> "Alas, my memory
> Does not want to leave me.
> And in it, live beings
> Each with its own pain,
> Each with its own dying,
> Its own trepidation."

The words seemed to come from Tomek's own heart as much as from his lips:

> "Don't think, don't remember
> The death on the cross,
> Though every day He dies,
> The only one, all-loving,
> Who without any need
> Consented and allowed
> To exist all that is,
> Including nails of torture.
>
> Totally enigmatic.
> Impossibly intricate.
> Better to stop speech here.
> This language is not for people.
> Blessed by jubilation.
> Vintages and harvests.
> Even if not everyone
> Is granted serenity."

She drifted off to sleep with Tomek's voice surrounding her.

Eva woke to a *ping*ing. The windows shook, and the *ping, ping* grew louder.

She sat up straight and listened. It had to be rain, but the noise sounded more like rocks on the roof.

There was no sign of Tomek, but murmuring voices came from the other end of the room, by the stove. It made her think of mornings at her grandmother's when she and her cousins slept on the couch just outside the kitchen. Eva had loved waking to the low voices and the gentle clinking of early breakfast preparations.

She lay down and drifted back to sleep.

When she awoke again, the smell of coffee and fresh-baked bread drifted in on a cold breeze. She shivered and started to burrow under the blanket again when she remembered. *The plums!*

She threw off the covers and raced to the window. Light came through the glass pane, but she couldn't see outside. The whole window was covered with a lace of ice, like a frosty map or a doily, icy cold to touch. Frost. Or worse.

Eva pulled on her boots at the front door and stepped out into the frigid wet air. Winter had come overnight and taken away colors, leaving the world wrapped in glittering, clear ice.

"Your orchards!" she cried.

"Eva? Come inside!" called Tomek's father, who had moved to the doorway behind her.

"Eva?" Pani Muchowiecka called from the kitchen.

Their voices sounded calm. But the ice—the hard, hard frost—must have meant they'd lost everything.

Ignoring their shouts, Eva ran down the hill toward the orchards. Maybe, just maybe, the ice missed the valley. Sleet pelted her cheeks, and she had to squint to keep it from stinging her eyes as her boots cracked shards of ice.

Just over the hill she got her answer. She broke to a walk. The orchards had been transformed into an icy wonderland. She walked between the rows, staring up at a ceiling of ice, branches sparkling like diamonds.

In front of her something dropped with a soft thud. She picked it up. The purple plum was perfectly encased in a cover of ice, which even as she held it began to melt.

Eva felt a hand on her shoulder. "Come," Tomek said softly. "My mother has breakfast."

They walked back together, past the ice-covered cross, Eva still holding the frozen plum, while behind them sounded the *thud, thud* of the family's falling fortune.

Tomek's mother was waiting with dry clothes. She handed Eva a heavy tan sweater and Eva's jeans from the day before, washed and dried.

Eva shivered, trying not to cry as she dressed in the tiny bathroom and splashed water on her face. When she came out, the others sat at the table, and she joined them.

"Lord," Papa said loud enough for the angels, "we do not understand what you did to your plums, but that is your business. For the food before us and your blessings, we thank you."

At first Eva couldn't speak. She waited for them to talk about the storm, what they would do now, what a disaster this was. Instead, Tomek and his father teased his mother about the first time she'd tried to cook bigos for her own mother, who had finally come to visit them from Lublin after fifteen years.

Eva glanced at them as the chatter grew even more lively.

Tomek smiled and kept the conversation going as he put jam on bread and passed it. His mother never ate, as far as Eva could tell. She kept moving about the kitchen, washing bowls, setting out fresh bread, opening a can of pâté or paste, touching Papa's shoulder slightly as she walked past.

And Papa, who had just lost at least half of his income overnight, had never looked more like jolly old Saint Nicholas.

As hard as it was to figure them out, Eva found it even harder not to be drawn into their mood, as if pulled under an umbrella in the middle of a rainstorm. The kitchen smelled like the orchard, the scent of plums filling spaces between air.

"*Smacznego!*" Pani Muchowiecka said, setting down a plate of freshly baked, bread-covered plums.

Eva recognized her own handiwork, the only lopsided pierogi. Reaching for the worst-looking one, she said, "I think I'll take this gorgeous one."

Papa laughed and made a pyramid of plum pierogi on her plate until Tomek burst out laughing and even Eva had to grin.

They ate plum pierogi, which Eva had to admit were the best things she'd ever eaten.

"Eva likes!" Papa said in English. "You have in America, Eva?"

Eva had never seen them. "They will when I get back," she promised. "I'll make them for all my friends." She thought about Matt and Melanie and wondered how she'd ever be able to explain this breakfast, this family.

As they cleared the table, Eva whispered to Tomek, "I had a great time. Your family is so . . . so wonderful, Tomek."

He grinned at her, his face slightly flushed.

Eva felt guilty. If she ever wanted Tomek to open up to her, she had to be honest with him. "Thank you for letting me come, Tomek." She took a deep breath and made herself say it. "I didn't do it to be helpful. I just wanted to get out of kitchen duty." She glanced up to see if he was going to get mad at her.

He slapped his cheeks. "I am shocked!" But he obviously wasn't. He must have known from the minute she'd asked to come.

Eva punched him in the shoulder. "You're so smart, aren't you, Tomek? Anyway, in spite of *you*, I'm awfully glad I came." She swallowed hard. "And I'm so sorry about the plums. If I could—"

Tomek held up his hand and frowned. His dad stopped talking, too. His mother gasped and put her hand over her mouth.

Outside a car door slammed. Then another.

They didn't move. They didn't breathe.

Boots crunched to the door. Someone knocked. Three times.

"I will answer," Tomek whispered.

More knocks, so loud the door shook.

Tomek lifted the latch and opened the door.

Three men in militia uniforms stormed in past him. The biggest one, his chest broad and his face round and red, with a brush mustache, shouted, "Muchowieckis, you are under arrest!"

→ 18 ←

Tomek glanced out the front door before shutting it behind the three policemen. There were others. He glimpsed
two cars, one with two militia keeping the motor running.
He turned to the three in his father's house and recognized
the oldest man, the one who had spoken. Pan Józef Krysa
had watched their house the year after Tadeusz's murder.
Tomek had heard that the old man had been promoted to
captain of the local unit.

"Pan Krysa," Tomek said, positioning himself between the men and Eva, "there must be some mistake."

The youngest soldier, his face as smooth as soap,
stepped forward, his hand on his holster.

Krysa ignored Tomek and turned to Papa. The two
older men were probably the same age, but the officer's
eyebrows had turned white; and under his fur cap, gray
hair stuck out. Built like a tank, Tomek's father used to

say, Krysa still carried broad shoulders and a fit appearance, except for his crooked nose, which must have been broken at least once.

"There is no mistake," said the captain. "You received official notice last month, Pan Muchowiecki, from the mayor himself. You were required to deliver twelve pigs for the good of our cause."

"That's not fair!" Eva cried.

She'd said it in English. Tomek glared at her. *Invisible, Eva. Be invisible.*

His father stepped in front of his mother, one hand behind his back, holding hers. "As you know, Captain Krysa, I do not raise pigs. I have never raised pigs, nor has any man in this county, to my knowledge."

Tomek's father had not told him about this controversy. The militia did not have absolute power in Poland. They needed an excuse for their cruelty, and this captain had chosen pigs.

"Pardon me," Tomek said, forcing his voice to stay even, "what is the fine for failing to deliver these pigs?"

The man stuck out his bottom lip in a false pout. "Your father knows he is already fined for late delivery— half of his plums."

"Half of his plums?" Tomek couldn't hold back the raging in his chest. "You can't—!"

His father took him by the arm and squeezed. "Tomek."

Tomek stopped. His head buzzed with his anger. This fine was wrong, unfair. His father was a good man, hardworking, generous. And he'd lost a son. Tomek felt Papa's grip on his arm tighten.

Forcing a laugh, Papa said, "Too bad for us all that the ice has taken half of our half, eh?"

The captain's mouth hardened into a thin line. Tomek could see years of hatred behind his murky black eyes. "Stefan Muchowiecki, you have been found negligent in your duties to our country and our allies. You will be punished and denied your state's generous allotment of coal for one year."

Tomek exploded. "A year without coal? How will they survive?" All the villagers depended on the coal allotment, meager as it was, to warm their homes and cook their meals. He pushed past the young punk of a soldier and stood nose to nose with his father's longtime enemy. "You can't leave them without heat all winter!"

The third soldier, a short fat man perhaps the age Tadeusz would have been, said, "He should have thought of that when he refused our honorable state!"

"Get out of here!" Tomek shouted.

"Tomek, don't!" Eva cried.

"Tomek!" His father reached for Tomek's arm, but Tomek shook it off.

"Get out of this house!" Tomek demanded.

The red-faced captain spit on the floor. "You are no better than your brother. We will leave now. As for you, Tomek Muchowiecki, you are to come with us! *You* are the one we have come to arrest."

"Not my son!" cried Papa.

Captain Krysa signaled to the other two militia. They rushed at Tomek and grabbed his arms.

Tomek struggled. The fat soldier elbowed him in the face.

Eva screamed.

"Józef, please!" begged his father.

Tomek felt the blood trickle down his nose. He had to keep control. He gazed at Eva, her face drawn into an agony of contortions as his father held her back. Tomek fought his urge to kick, to bite, to kill. And he stopped. He stopped fighting, stopped struggling. If they took him, only him, he could handle this. He had to get them away from Eva and from his parents. Tomek let himself be dragged backward to the door.

Outside, one of the militia forced Tomek's arms behind his back and snapped on handcuffs. He heard the engine of the second police car start up. They jerked him around, forcing his head against the car door, and shoved him into the backseat of the Fiat Polski. It smelled like vomit and sweat.

They took off fast, back wheels slipping. Tomek tried to look back, and the short guard hit him on the head and laughed.

From the front seat Captain Krysa turned around and again stuck out his bottom lip. "So, my little Muchowiecki, you have found yourself in some very big trouble this time. Do not worry. I and your father go back a long ways. I will try to help you. But you must try to help me look good to my bosses. Yes?"

Tomek didn't answer. He would have taken a dozen like the fat soldier or the young one over this old militia officer, the sworn enemy of his father. He prayed that his mother would be able to keep Papa from coming to the police station. Krysa would like nothing better than to have an excuse to interrogate Stefan Muchowiecki. Not that he had not tried before. Twice that Tomek knew of, the captain, not yet promoted, had arrested and detained his father. But the outcry from the village had been sudden and furious, and they had released him.

"So, you do not answer me, Tomek Muchowiecki?" Krysa snorted a laugh. "Very well. You will talk to me sooner or later."

The rest of the drive, Tomek stared out the window, shutting out their crude, sporadic conversations. When the car stopped, the two militia in the car behind them joined the others, as if Tomek needed five guards. The other two had blue-gray uniforms, much nicer and warmer than the local uniforms. They said something to the captain, then got back into their Fiat and drove off.

Tomek didn't struggle as they led him up the steps and into the police station. He had been inside the musty office many times to register his presence with the authorities, and each time it struck him how isolated this place was. The building sat by itself, with no houses in sight and only one tree a distance from the A-framed wood office. In the small central room, the captain's office, a coal furnace blazed.

"Take him to the interrogation room!" Captain Krysa ordered.

The two militia dragged him down a short hallway and threw him into a tiny room. Tomek fell on his arm, sprawling facedown on the cement floor, cold and stained with rust-colored splotches. He felt like vomiting. He imagined his brother, gentle fervent Tadeusz, in this cell with men like these. How could nothing have changed?

After all these years, with men like Tadeusz dying for a better Poland, here he was.

A cockroach scurried in front of him, inches from his ear. Tomek drew himself up and scooted back across the floor, which felt damp, growing wetter toward the walls. The room smelled like a urinal, sour and foul. Walls and ceiling were rough gray stone like the floor, a concrete tomb with only an overhead lightbulb, a tiny table, and two straight-backed, wooden chairs.

The door opened.

Tomek felt his heart lunge as the two militia, the fat and the young one, came back in without their coats, their shirtsleeves rolled up. The young officer reminded Tomek of a deer he and Tadeusz had spotted in the orchards, caught in a tangle of wire. The boy's eyes darted from Tomek to the other guard.

The fat one carried a wooden bat, which he smacked into his palm as he crouched down, eye-level with Tomek. "I knew your brother."

Tomek wanted to hurl himself at the man, to ram him into the wall over and over and over until there was nothing left of him. He bit his cheek, hard, feeling the blood warm his mouth. He couldn't lose his temper. He couldn't give them an excuse.

The disgusting fat man stood up, his shirt half tucked in and half out. "You may as well talk while you can."

Tomek didn't answer. But being invisible was no longer an option.

The young militia shuffled about the room, not looking at Tomek.

"Where are you registered?" The fat officer hovered over him, so all Tomek could see was the big belly and a tiny head above it.

"*Uniwersytet Łódzki,*" he answered. "I would get you the paper, but my hands are tied."

The man frowned, apparently unsure whether he'd been insulted or not. "Why are you not there now, citizen?"

Tomek had decided it would be safer not to register with the local authorities in Brzegi and arouse suspicion. They never should have found out he was with his parents. Someone must have told them. He waited. He would interrogate this fat militia in his own way. He would find out what they already knew.

"My father needed me for his harvest," Tomek said. His nose itched, and he longed to scratch it.

"What do you know about Zakopane?" the guard asked, pulling the chair in front of Tomek and straddling it backward. His nose ran, and he wiped it on his bare arm.

Tomek tried to swallow, but his mouth had gone dry. How could they know about Zakopane? *What* did they know? The militia could not have found out already unless someone had betrayed them.

"Well, Muchowiecki?" The guard tapped the wooden bat against the chair leg. *Tap. Tap.* The sound echoed in the small room.

Tomek tried not to think of his brother. Of his brother's injured knee. Instead, he turned all his thoughts to Eva. She was so beautiful, and never more beautiful than when she had tried to stop them from arresting him. "Zakopane? What do I know of Zakopane?"

The fat guard's eyes became tiny bullets in mounds of fleshy fat. "Yes! Zakopane!"

"Very good skiing," Tomek said.

The guard stood up so fast the chair tipped over. "You will answer me!" He lifted the bat and swung it down with both hands.

Tomek rolled just in time to take the blow on his thigh. It stung with waves of pain. He imagined Eva on skis, her hair blowing wild behind her.

"We know all about the American professor, the friend of the rebel priest!" shouted the fat man. "Who is behind this? What are they planning to do?"

Tomek saw the bat smack against the man's palm again, heard the slap of wood against flesh, fought the image of his brother sitting on this same cement floor. Tomek could tell them what he knew. They already had the answers. Someone had betrayed the group. Why should he keep silent for nothing? Lose an eye or a leg . . . or worse?

"I asked you question!" the fat officer screamed.

What would Tadeusz do? The old question came as it had done years ago, naturally, automatically. And with it came the answer: *Do what is best for God and for Poland.*

"Why are you smiling?" roared the officer. "Something is funny?"

"Nothing is funny," Tomek said quietly.

The man slapped him, and Tomek fell backward, knocking his head on the cement floor. "Answer me! What does the American teach? Where are the rest of you? What are you planning?" He kicked Tomek in the back.

Tomek felt the pain rip up his spine. But he wasn't

there. He was deep inside of himself, where God was, where Poland filled places behind his skin, protecting his heart as the kicks kept coming. He could keep sinking, moving farther away with every blow, lost in the depths of where he was.

"Stop, Arkadiusz! You will kill him!" The young militia's voice trembled.

The door creaked open. Tomek heard boots on the cement.

"Leave us." The quiet voice of Captain Krysa sounded far away. "We must talk like civilized men, Muchowiecki. To reason together."

Tomek felt as if he were floating to the surface, bubbling up from the depths of the Baltic Sea. His breath came in shallow gasps, as a fish struggling on the shore, half in, half out. He imagined Eva in the plum orchard, racing Łukasz, her slender fingers urging the plums off the branches.

"Sit. Sit at this table. We talk as men." The captain pulled Tomek's arm.

Tomek jerked away from him. The movement caused a stabbing pain in his side. Holding his breath against the pain, he managed to pull himself to a sitting position. The room spun. He closed his eyes until it stopped. Reaching across for the empty chair, he hauled himself into it.

That's when he saw something shiny on the table, a silver metal box. A briefcase or a toolbox.

"You must believe me when I tell you I do not want to use these tools." The captain's voice betrayed him, his eagerness spilling out of his eyes and mouth. "Now, what are you up to, Muchowiecki?"

"Picking plums."

"A plum picker?" He clicked the locks on the silver case.

Tomek knew the Soviet-trained militia had perfected implements of torture. Shock treatments and cattle prods showed up with militia to dispel striking workers. And there were worse things, things never spoken of.

Krysa scooted his chair closer to the table. The deafening screech filled the room.

Tomek waited, forcing himself not to imagine the tools of torture that waited for him in that silver case. Closing his eyes, he guided his mind back to the bus ride from Zakopane with Eva. He could almost feel her head on his shoulder as she talked about her mother. He'd wanted to wrap her in his arms and never let her go.

Why hadn't he opened up to her as she had to him? He had wanted to, longed to unload his confusion about Tadeusz, about what his brother had fought and died for. But Eva was American. And beautiful.

Yet Eva had opened herself to him. And he had kept quiet, afraid to break the spell of Eva, afraid if he cracked himself open she would not like what poured out.

Watching the way Eva was with his family, with his father and mother and Stash, Tomek had begun to feel things he had not wanted to feel. How she moved him! When Tadeusz had died, a piece of Tomek had died with him. The hopeful part. He felt this. How could he risk loving and losing again, letting another piece of himself die? If he did this, he might disappear altogether.

Eva was a rich American girl with an American boyfriend, a daughter of a professor. She would leave his country the first chance she got. Since Nowa Huta he had done his best to stay away from her. But in Brzegi, as he watched her breathe new life into his mother and father, Tomek had lost his will, no longer able to help himself from falling in love with her.

Krysa was asking him something, shouting perhaps, but Tomek could not hear the words. Again he pictured Eva, her fair skin, the way her eyes changed colors when she got angry. He let himself be drawn into those eyes, until he went under and felt nothing but blackness.

⊷ 19 ⊷

Eva fought off panic as she stared at the militia station, imagining what they might be doing to Tomek at this very minute. She had no idea how long she and Łukasz had been sitting in his truck, parked across the street, neither of them daring to speak.

Tomek's father had run to Łukasz's house as soon as the militia left, and Łukasz had driven over immediately. It had taken all of them to keep Pan Muchowiecki from storming the militia office himself. But in the end, his wife had convinced him with her quiet wisdom. "Krysa does this to get at you, Stefan. Do not let him win."

Łukasz's fingers drummed the steering wheel. Then he pounded his fist. "I should go in there! This should not happen, not again. Not to Tomek!"

Eva put her hand on his arm. "Łukasz, you'll only make things worse. You said so yourself—to Tomek's father. Please! I need you here with me. We'll get Tomek out of there. We have to. But we can't—"

The door to the police station opened, and three officers stepped out, their laughter coming with them. They were dragging something in the middle of them. With growing terror Eva realized it was Tomek.

Without thinking, Eva flung open the truck door and jumped out to the street.

"Eva!" Łukasz shouted behind her.

Her foot slipped, and she nearly fell on the icy road. But she got her balance and ran across. A streak of sunlight parted the clouds, falling on Tomek's still, lifeless body. Eva stumbled across the police yard toward him.

The fat soldier looked up. *"Stać! Nie wolno!"*

Eva ignored him and ran straight to Tomek, dropping to her knees. He lay curled on his side, dried blood on his cheek, matted in his hair. "Tomek!" She pressed her face to his, felt his breath. He was alive. "Tomek," she whispered.

Above her, Polish words were exchanged. Feet shuffled. Someone bumped her shoulder. She hugged Tomek, lifting his head from the ground.

His eyes fluttered.

"Tomek! I'm here. It's Eva. Wake up!"

She heard footsteps behind her and turned to see Łukasz, a blurry shadow through her tears.

"We take my cousin home now," Łukasz said.

"Maybe we have questions for *you*!" snapped the fat militia.

Łukasz pushed past him.

Tomek's eyes opened. He frowned at Eva, shut his eyes, and opened them again. "Eva? Get away—!"

Captain Krysa sighed. "I am weary of Muchowieckis. Get him out of here." He strode back to the station, his boot brushing Tomek as he passed.

"The handcuffs!" Eva shouted after him. "Take them off!"

Without turning around, Krysa raised his hand and snapped his fingers. Then he stepped inside.

The young officer unlocked Tomek's handcuffs. Then he scurried after his captain, leaving only the fat officer, who let out a harsh laugh before trailing inside after the others.

"We must leave now," Łukasz said, bending to help Tomek off the ground.

Tomek groaned and reached for his head.

"Łukasz is here," Eva whispered, slipping her arm around Tomek's waist and lifting his arm over her shoulder. Łukasz did the same from the other side, and they moved toward the truck. Tomek tried to walk, but something was wrong with his leg. She tried not to think of Tadeusz, of what they might have done to Tomek's knees.

"We're almost there," she whispered as they crossed the street.

"You shouldn't . . . ," Tomek mumbled, his voice trailing off.

"We're okay, Tomek," Eva said, not daring to look behind them. "Everything's going to be all right." She could barely move under his weight, and her feet slipped on the ice as they reached the truck.

Łukasz took over, lifting Tomek's body into the truck, pushing his feet in after him.

Eva climbed in between them. "Go! Get us out of here!"

The engine started. Tires squealed. The truck swerved, then bounced onto the road.

"Do you think he's okay, Łukasz?" Eva asked, when the militia station was out of sight and they were headed east, back to Tomek's home. "He's not unconscious, is he?" She stared at his eyelids. They twitched, as if his eyes were watching something only he could see. She leaned into his face and felt his steady breathing. "I think he's just asleep, don't you?"

"He will survive." Łukasz held the steering wheel with one hand and squirmed out of his jacket. "Take this." He shoved it at her. "You are shivering."

Eva took the jacket but placed it over Tomek. Wiping the blood off his forehead, she whispered, "What have they done to you?"

Tomek jerked in the seat. "Stop!" His eyes focused. He shook his head and sat up straighter. For a minute, he didn't speak. He glanced across Eva to Łukasz, as if trying to remember where he was. "They know . . . about Zakopane," he muttered. "They asked me. Zakopane. They know."

"*Shhh.*" Eva studied Tomek. She didn't want to think about anything except the fact that Tomek was here, next to her. He was hurt. That much was obvious. But she didn't think it was his knee. The leg bent squarely as he sat up. He held his side, as if a rib might have been broken or bruised. "Are you all right, Tomek?" she asked, her finger touching his cheek, rubbing away the last of the blood.

Tomek stared into her eyes without looking away as he usually did. He put his arms around her and pulled her into him, hugging her hard. "I am all right, Eva Lott. *We* are all right."

Tomek's mother wasted no tears when she saw her son. Eva watched as the stoic woman set about the business of inspecting and bandaging his wounds. "The ribs are not broken," she pronounced, "though not for want of trying."

Tomek sat unflinching through alcohol and taping. When his mother had finished, he stood up. Immediately his hand went to the chair to steady himself.

"You must leave soon," said his father. "Old Józef will find another excuse to detain you. He can keep you detained for three days, then move you to another station for three more days, and so on for as long as they wish. It will be safer for you in Zakopane."

"Zakopane." Tomek pushed himself from the chair. "I need to warn them." He turned to his father. "But what about you? If they don't give you the coal allotment—" Tomek winced as he sat back down and reached for his boot.

"We will find our way," Papa promised. "You are not to worry about that."

Łukasz had sat quietly on the couch while Tomek's

wounds were being bandaged. Now he went to his cousin and took over lacing his boots. "I will chop enough wood for your family, Tomek."

"They've made it illegal to chop wood in our own forest, Łukasz!" Tomek shouted. "They would arrest you."

"God will provide, Tomek," his father said quietly. He turned and winked at his wife. "He always has."

Eva wanted to think like that, to believe like that. She knew her mother had. And she, herself, had believed, had hoped . . . *before*. Eva gazed at Tomek's mother, her gentle calm almost contagious. Staring into this strong woman's eyes, Eva could almost believe the promise of the woman's husband, that God would provide.

A thumping came from the side of the house.

Eva gasped.

Tomek held up his hand for them to be quiet.

Eva moved in beside Tomek. She could hear his and Łukasz's breathing, something creaking in the kitchen, the wind howling outside, and something else, a sound coming closer, growing louder.

⤏ 20 ⤎

The sound came again, longer—*thump, thump, thump, thump, thump*—like acorns dropping.

Papa tiptoed to the window, rubbed off the fog with his sleeve, and stared out, his nose to the glass. *"Boże mój!"* he muttered.

"What is it?" Eva whispered.

Tomek limped to the window, and Eva followed, wedging herself between Tomek and his dad. In the yard she saw someone she recognized, one of the cousins or neighbors from the orchard. He was walking away.

Papa tapped on the window.

The man turned around, waved, and kept walking.

Another man, much older and as thin as Piotrek in Nowa Huta, passed him, strolling toward the house, hands in pockets. Behind him came the woman who had carried a basket for *obiad* in the orchard field. Next to her, little

Stash walked heel-to-toe, his arms out at his sides, as if he were walking a tightrope.

Tomek's mother and Łukasz pressed in closer, peering over and around Eva to see out the window.

"What's happening?" Łukasz asked.

"I will find out!" Papa said, heading for the door.

They all trailed him outside. Slanted sunlight cast a long shadow, landing on the worn cross, making it glow as if it were on fire. With no coats, they jogged to the side of the house.

Stash stood by the cellar and turned his pockets inside out. Three pieces of coal dropped, *thump, thump, thump,* into the coal bin, joining a small pile already there.

"Stasiek?" Tomek's mother called.

The woman Eva took to be Stash's mother stepped up beside him and unfolded her apron, letting drop several pieces of coal.

A young girl dashed up behind them, grinned at Tomek, then emptied her purse, which was filled with lumps of coal. As quickly as she'd appeared, she disappeared back into the fields.

"We heard of the misfortune," Stash's mother explained.

"We're taking turns!" Stash shouted.

"I don't understand," Papa said.

"You will not be in want, friends," answered Stash's mother. "Your neighbors will see to that each day."

Stash's smile took up half his face. "For the whole winter!"

Eva ran up and took Stash into her arms. Their neighbors, who barely received enough coal to warm their own homes, were sharing what little they had with Tomek's family. She twirled Stash in a circle, pressing her cheek to his hair. He smelled like coal, wonderful, beautiful coal.

When Stash's family had gone, Eva and Tomek got ready for the trek back to Zakopane. Łukasz volunteered to drive them to the bus stop, and Eva thanked him before Tomek could claim he didn't need a ride.

At the door, Papa hugged both of them, crushing them together inside his strong arms. "You come back soon, Eva Lott. Take care of my boy."

Eva clung to his hand. "Thank you . . . for everything." How could she begin to tell him what the last two days had meant to her? She squeezed his calloused fingers. *"Do widzenia, Papa."*

Tomek's mother brought them a brown bag and hugged her son. She checked the bandage she'd wound around his chest, inspected the bandages on his head.

Then she turned to Eva. She reached into her apron pocket and came out with a small object wrapped in brown paper. Hugging Eva, Pani Muchowiecka rattled something in Polish, so low Eva couldn't pick up anything except "thank you."

Eva turned to Tomek for help.

"My mother says thank you, and you are to take this gift with you."

Eva removed the paper and stared at the pocked, rough plum pit in her palm.

Tomek continued, "My mother says that in this plum pit is the essence of the plum. It is the same as it was yesterday—no less, though the outside is stripped away so you cannot see red or purple or taste its sweetness. The inside is unchanged."

His mother whispered something to Tomek and nodded for him to interpret. Eva didn't want to miss a word. "My mother says this is the heart of the orchard. You are to think of this as the heart, the pit of Poland, and remember."

Eva closed her fingers around the rough pit. Then she hugged Tomek's mother, feeling the warmth of the woman's soft plump arms enfold her. How long had it been since she'd felt a hug reach inside of her? Eva's mother had hugged like this before the cancer wasted her body. Even after her mother had lost so much weight that Eva outweighed her, Eva had longed for those weak hugs that were somehow the same inside, like this hug. A heart hug.

"We better go," Łukasz said.

Eva let go of Pani Muchowiecka. She wasn't sure she understood about the pit, about the heart, but she knew she'd been handed a secret, a hard-fought secret, a glimpse of hope.

"*Dziękuję,*" Eva said, fighting a waver in her voice. They made for Łukasz's truck, scaring up a gathering of blackbirds, who took off from bare branches in unison, forming dozens of tiny black crosses against the sky.

———

On the bus ride home while Tomek slept, Eva kept checking her pocket to make sure the plum pit was still there. She was going back to kitchen duty, to cold sheets, to bread with something on it, and quite possibly to danger in Zakopane. But she knew nothing would be the same, not ever.

As they neared Zakopane, she stared at the black night outside the bus window and thought about what Tomek's mother had said, about the plum pit, about the heart of Poland. She closed her eyes and let her head rest on Tomek's shoulder. He slept so soundly.

She turned to look at his face again, the swollen nose and bandaged brow. His deep-set eyes were handsome, even when shut. Stretching toward him, she leaned up and kissed his lips, lightly, softly. He didn't stir.

As the bus bounced over the rough road through town, Eva stuck her hand into her pocket and closed her fingers around the plum pit, feeling the warmth of a hug as she squeezed her gift hard enough to mark her palm.

When the bus ground to a stop, Eva helped Tomek down the bus steps and on down the hill toward Widokówka. Stars broke through the black sky, giving them enough light to see their way clearly. "I never thought I'd be happy to get back to kitchen duty," she said, laughing easily. An owl hooted from a nearby tree. "I miss my little dog."

She missed her dad, too. But it might make her sound like a little girl to admit it. And the last thing she wanted was for Tomek Muchowiecki to think of her as a little girl. It had to be after midnight, and they hadn't planned to stay one night in Brzegi, much less two. Her father would be worried, but nothing like he would have been if he'd known what had gone on during the last twenty-four hours.

Tomek had been leaning on her. Now he stopped. Eva turned and gazed up at him. Moonlight brushed across his face. Even bandaged and bruised, it was a handsome face, with strong cheekbones and a firm jaw.

"Eva Lott . . ." He glanced at the stars, then back into her eyes. "You are very brave." His mouth moved into a slight grin. "And not a bad kisser . . . for an American girl."

"You—!" He hadn't been asleep on the bus! He'd been wide awake when she'd kissed him. "For an American girl, huh?" She hoped she sounded angry, instead of beyond embarrassed. "How'd you like to race this American girl down the hill, tough guy?"

Tomek smiled, then reached out and held her head in his hands.

She closed her eyes and felt his breath as he moved closer. Then she felt his lips, full and gentle, moving in little kisses from her forehead to her nose to her cheek, her chin. He covered her lips with his, kissing her, slow and deep. She could have melted into him.

They held hands the rest of the way to Widokówka. The night was still. Eva had never known such absolute silence, as if they were the only two people left on earth.

No outside lights shone from Widokówka, so they sneaked inside like normal American teens out past curfew on a Friday night. Eva hung their coats on the wall pegs, then heard the clicking of toenails on the stairs.

"Samson!"

The ball of fluff leaped two steps and jumped into Eva's arms. "Good dog! I missed you!" She buried her face in his fur, feeling as if they'd been apart for weeks.

"I'm jealous," Tomek said.

"Of Samson or me?"

A door creaked open, followed by footsteps down the hallway. Then Grażyna came down the stairs in socks and bathrobe. "You are back!" Her red hair fell in two thin, fuzzy braids.

Eva set Samson down. "Barely."

Grażyna stopped on the bottom step, next to Eva. She squinted at Tomek. "What happened to you?"

"The militia happened to him," Eva began.

Tomek stopped her, his voice stiff, frigid. "What is it, Grażyna? Something has happened. Tell me."

Eva glanced at Tomek. Lines cut into his forehead as he stared past her to Grażyna. Eva felt her body shudder and the air drain from the room.

Above them, more footsteps sounded on the stairs. Anna descended, fully dressed. "Who is it, Grażyna? What do they want?" She stopped when she saw who it was. "Tomek!" She turned on Eva and glared, her lip curled in disgust, in hatred.

"Eva!" Krystyna trotted down the stairs. Crying, she threw her arms around Eva.

Eva couldn't stop trembling. She yelled up the stairs, "Dad? Dad!"

There was no answer.

Breathless, as if poised at the top of a roller coaster, a second from the crashing descent, Eva took Krystyna by the shoulders. "Where's my father? Krystyna, where is he?"

Gasping between sobs, Krystyna managed to get the words out: "He is not here. Oh, Eva! They have taken your father!"

"No!" Eva screamed. She shook Krystyna. "Where is he? *Who* took him? Where did they take him?"

But Krystyna could only cry louder and mutter, "The militia."

Eva stumbled backward. "I . . . I'm going to him." Her coat. She'd need her coat. She'd have to walk. Her mind raced, blurring her thoughts. She dashed to the wall peg, yanked down her coat, and tried to put her arms in the sleeves. Wildly, she tore at it, searching for the armholes.

"Eva, don't," Tomek said, taking her arm. She shook him off.

"Your father will be fine." Grażyna's voice was so calm, as if fathers were taken every day. "Father Blachnicki will see that no harm comes to him."

"Father Blachnicki? Father B. is with my dad?" She couldn't have said which language she was speaking in. If her father was with the priest, then he was all right. He'd have to be all right.

Tomek put his arm around Eva. "Tell us exactly what happened, Grażyna."

"Father B. arrived last night," Grażyna explained. "He warned us that we had been betrayed, that the militia knew all about our activities."

"I knew it!" Tomek interrupted. He nodded for Grażyna to go on.

"Father B. had word that the militia possessed orders to expel from Poland the American professor. As soon as Pani Kurczak heard this, she took off for her villa in Gydnia."

"But Father B. stayed until the militia came," Krystyna added. "He vowed not to abandon your father, Eva."

Eva imagined her father waiting with the old Polish priest. Waiting for what?

Grażyna continued, "The militia arrived minutes after this. They looked at Professor Lott's visa and said it was not in order and he must leave the country immediately, that they will drive him to the Austrian border."

"But what if they didn't?" Eva cried. "What if they arrested him? What if he's in their prison right now and—?"

"No, Eva," Krystyna said. "Father B. went with them in the militia car. He will not let this happen."

"Father B. went with them? To Austria?" Tomek asked.

"To Austria, to Rome," Anna snapped. "He has left Poland."

"Rome?" Tomek repeated.

Anna made a spitting noise with her lips. "Have you not heard? Blachnicki believes the next pope will be Polish, his friend Wojtyła. He would not miss being there when it happens, no matter what is going on in his own country."

Eva had trouble focusing. Her head felt waterlogged. "But what if the militia lied?"

"Father B. is very powerful, Eva," Tomek explained. "And your father is American. They will not detain him."

"But even if they really drive to the border, then what? They just drop my father in the middle of nowhere?"

"Father B. knows many people in Vienna," Tomek assured her, tightening his arm around her shoulders, as if that could keep her from shattering into pieces. "They will be anxious to help. Father B. will not let anything happen to your father. They will both be safe."

"Yes, yes," Anna said, her voice harsh. "Your American father will be fine. Father B. will see to the professor. But what about Andrzej? Who will see to him?"

"Andrzej?" Tomek asked. "What about Andrzej?"

"He's being detained," Grażyna answered.

"But why? Why Andrzej?" Eva could picture his impish grin. Of all the students in Zakopane, he had the sweetest spirit.

Anna threw her hands in the air. "It is a false arrest! They have made up an offense. They say that Andrzej is the one who painted pink their precious statue of Lenin."

"They took him for that?" Eva asked. "He was just playing a joke."

They all turned and stared at her.

"What do you know about this?" Anna demanded. "Andrzej did not do it."

"Well, yeah . . . he did," Eva admitted. She didn't see what harm it could do to say so now. "But so what? They can't arrest him for that, can they?"

"You knew about it?" Tomek asked. His arm slid away from her.

Eva glanced from Tomek to Anna to Grażyna to Krystyna and back to Tomek. "The night he did it, he came to our room and told Dad. He was afraid he might have drawn attention to us. He wanted to know what to do. Dad told him not to tell anybody."

She caught the look that passed between Anna and Tomek. And she didn't like it. "What? What's the matter?"

Quietly, Grażyna said, "We did not think any of us knew this information."

"So?" She tried to get Tomek to look at her. "Tell me!"

Anna glared at Eva as she said, "No one knew Andrzej painted that statue, except you and your father. And now, the militia. Father B. told us we have been betrayed. And now we know who betrayed us."

→ 21 ←

"Betrayed us? Me?" Eva cried. "That's crazy . . ." But she couldn't grab the right words, the Polish words. *A traitor? Her?* And just when she felt she finally got it, got Poland, understood why her dad wanted to come to this country, believed herself that what they were doing in Zakopane mattered!

Her mind swirled as the anger boiled in her head, making it throb. "Don't look at me like that!" she shouted in English. "Tomek?"

She took a deep breath, collecting herself. This was unbelievable.

She grabbed Samson and hugged him to her chest, then shoved past Anna and Grażyna to the stairs. She didn't stop until she reached her room and slammed the door behind her.

But she could still see their faces, Krystyna's sad eyes, Anna's hatred. And Tomek?

She wanted her dad, missed him with the ache reserved for missing her mother. His jacket lay on the bed with his briefcase. His clothes still hung in the wardrobe. Yet the room felt totally empty, like their house after Mom died. Eva remembered coming back after the funeral and seeing her mother's purse beside a chair, her oven mitts in the kitchen, her coat still in the hall closet next to Eva's. It had felt like each object screamed that her mother was gone, that she'd never need any of these things again. That Eva would always be alone.

And now, her dad's pencil, his socks, his *torba*, all gave the same message.

Something white stuck out between the *torba* and coat on the bed. Eva walked over and picked it up. It was a note from Dad.

Someone knocked at her door. *Tomek?*

"Eva?" It was Krystyna. "Are you okay?"

"I need to be alone for a while, Krystyna," Eva said.

She felt Krystyna linger outside the door. Then her footsteps faded up the hall.

Eva unfolded the note from her father and read:

Eva, Not much time. They think I'm packing. I'm so sorry I got you into this, honey. Forgive me. Don't worry about me! Father B. is going with me to Vienna. I'll be fine. You'll be safe with Tomek until I can get you out. Stay safe.—Love, Dad

She read it again, imagining her dad's hand as he scrawled the letters. Some of the words, she could barely make out. They were shaky, not like his usual perfect handwriting. He must have been so scared, in such a hurry. She read it again.

A knock at the door made her jump.

"Not now, Krystyna, please?" she called.

"Eva?" Tomek's voice came in through the cracks of the door. "Let me in."

He should have rushed to her defense. He should have—

"Eva, I need to talk to you."

She stared at the door. "No," she said quietly. Her throat burned with tears she refused to let out.

"Don't be childish, Eva."

"*Childish?*" She grabbed the pillow off the bed and covered her ears with it. Still she heard the knocking. Dropping to the floor, she put her head on her dad's jacket and pulled the pillow so hard against her head she couldn't breathe.

When she sat up, the knocking had stopped. Eva reached into her coat pocket and brought out the plum pit Tomek's mother had given her. It felt as if Brzegi had happened years ago. She stared at the drying brown oval in her hand. Unable to hold back the flood of tears any longer, she burst into sobs.

The heart of Poland. Eva threw the pit across the room. They believed that *she* had betrayed *them?* They had it backward.

Tomek sat at the breakfast table, chewing bread that would not go down. He hadn't slept all night. Half the night he had sat on the staircase, guarding Eva from the militia, who might come to take her away.

"Do you think she will come down for breakfast?" Krystyna asked, as if reading his thoughts.

"Why should she?" Anna snapped. "Let the little traitor starve!"

"Eva is not the traitor. She would never betray Andrzej or any of us, even by accident. If you had seen her with Łukasz at the police station in Brzegi—"

"Yes, yes, yes." Anna's voice was filled with bitterness. She got up from the table and poured herself more *herbatka*. "So you have told us. Unfortunately, she is not so romantic for Andrzej as for you."

Tomek stood up so quickly, the table scooted. "She did not betray us!"

Anna turned cold, green eyes on him. "Then who did?"

Tomek looked away. "I don't know." He had gone over and over it in his head. Janek was the only student at Widokówka he didn't completely trust. Yet Janek would never betray the group at Zakopane to the militia he hated. Besides, Janek needed Father B.'s Oasis group for the printing press. In all of Poland, there were only two printing presses not owned by the government. Janek and his people used the press in Oasis possession to print their freedom bulletins. He would never risk losing that printer.

Pani Kurczak was another possibility. She was no

believer in their cause. But she made good money renting to groups under the table, receiving dollars she did not report. She had a good thing going in Zakopane. She would never turn herself in.

Tomek knew as well as anyone that every citizen of Poland was watched. But since he had arrived in Zakopane, since he had met Eva, he had gotten lazy, forgetting to search crowds for the watchers. His mind had become filled with other things—poetry, thoughts of his brother, Poland, . . . and Eva. He should have been paying attention.

Yet what was known about the Zakopane group could not have come from the outside. The militia knew about Andrzej and Professor Lott. And they had known about Tomek. He remembered the fleeting thought he'd had in that interrogation room, that someone close to them had betrayed them.

Anna was right about one thing. They *had* been betrayed. But as Tomek tried to piece things together, the only thing he was certain of was that Eva Lott was not the traitor. He had been too slow to think, slow to speak when Anna accused her. But he had never doubted Eva.

He had just about decided to walk into town and see if he could pick up news of militia activities in the area or word of Father B., when he heard someone calling from the front door.

"Hallo!" It sounded like Andrzej!

Tomek tore up the basement steps. "Andrzej!"

"*Cześć*, Tomek!" Andrzej stood in the doorway, his pajama top tucked into his brown pants. He took off his beret and bowed. "I was missed?"

Tomek and Krystyna rushed at Andrzej, nearly toppling him.

"What happened to you, Tomek? You look awful." Andrzej hadn't stopped smiling since he'd come in, but now his smile faded.

"I'm fine," Tomek assured him. "But you? Look at you! How did you get out?"

"Andrzej!" Eva cried from the top of the stairs. She raced down, pushed her way through, and wrapped her arms around his neck. "You're all right!"

Tomek thought that even in her jeans and sweatshirt, she looked more beautiful than he had ever seen her.

Andrzej, his cheeks pink as the Lenin statue, grinned at Tomek over Eva's head. "I will go away more often if this is the welcome greeting I will get on return!"

"Did they hurt you, Andrzej?" Anna asked, coming alongside Eva. She glared at Eva as she said, "We know all about the American traitor."

"The what?" Andrzej squinted at Anna, his nose wrinkled.

"She told us she and her father knew you were the one who painted Lenin," Anna explained.

Still, Andrzej looked puzzled. He scratched his beard. "Ah! And you thought *she* was the one who informed to the militia? Eva?"

Anna's irritation flashed in her eyes. She'd never

shown much patience with Andrzej or with Krystyna. "Of course, Eva! She betrayed you! She is a traitor!"

"*Nie!*" Andrzej shook his head. "Not Eva! It was Grażyna. I heard them say. She listens at the doors as she scrubs our floors. She is a watcher. I am sorry, Tomek."

Tomek should have felt surprise, shock. Grażyna had been Tadeusz's friend. Tomek had believed her to be his friend as well. But instead of surprise, he felt only a sickness in his stomach that made him want to retch.

"I was idiot to paint pink the statue of Lenin when I should risk only for more important matters." Andrzej's eyes looked watery, and he sounded serious for the first time since Tomek had known him. "So many things our government is doing to our people, things that no one will know without the free press. I want to help let them know."

Eva stood on tiptoes and kissed Andrzej's forehead. "I'm glad you're safe, Andrzej," she whispered. Then without looking at any of them, she pulled on her coat and stepped outside.

"Poor Eva," Krystyna muttered after the door closed.

"You must tell me what was done with the professor," Andrzej said.

Krystyna began a detailed explanation and had the men all the way to Vienna when Tomek's mind clicked in. "Where is Grażyna?" he asked, interrupting Krystyna's account. He tried to remember when he'd seen her last.

"She is still here?" Andrzej asked.

"She went to the market," Krystyna answered.

"That was hours ago!" Anna shouted.

Tomek ran to Grażyna's room, on the second floor. The door was locked, but he opened it with one kick.

The room was empty. Nothing hung in the wardrobe. Not a trace of his brother's friend had been left. He wanted to find her—not to hurt her or punish her, but to make her explain to him. Had she betrayed Tadeusz, too, so many years ago? Or had his death changed her so much? Tomek would probably never know. And if he did, he would never understand.

He needed to think, to put events together. He walked outside to clear his head. Andrzej was leaning against the old Renault, and Tomek settled beside him. "What now, Andrzej?" he asked. "What will happen because of Grażyna?"

Andrzej tugged his beret lower over his forehead. "For now, the militia have what they want. They have broken up our group. They are rid of the American professor. They must know all about Janek's black-market activities, though he is too quick for them and has disappeared. They know we have nothing at Widokówka, no printing press. What threat are we?"

This was all true, Tomek knew. Yet the militia would not forget about them. He believed Father B.'s people would eventually have to leave Widokówka.

Tomek gazed out at the Tatras. He thought he could make out the very peak where his brother had planted his cross. "What threat are we, Andrzej? I will tell you. We *are* a threat, my friend. They may not realize this yet, but we are a very great threat."

Suddenly, Andrzej stood up and squinted down the road. "Look! It's Krzysztof." Andrzej turned his back to the road and walked directly to the house without another word.

Tomek stayed where he was but pretended not to see the officer dressed in the tan uniform of the local brigade.

Krzysztof belonged to the militia and worked part-time at Zakopane headquarters. But what his bosses didn't know was that the rest of the time he was one of Father B.'s couriers. Like many of the militia, Krzysztof had shown up at the back door of Father B.'s church one morning and asked that his baby be baptized. Since then, he had smuggled in mail for people like Professor Lott throughout southern Poland. He had brought in the few letters the Lotts had received.

Krzysztof ignored Tomek as he crossed the yard to the old tree at the corner. He kicked the trunk and circled its broad branches. Then he left.

As soon as Krzysztof was out of sight, Tomek retrieved two items from a hole in the largest branch—a letter for Father B. and a telegram for Eva.

Andrzej was waiting inside. Tomek handed him the letter with Father B.'s name scribbled on the outside in pencil.

Andrzej turned the letter over and over. "What should we do? This could be important. We don't know when Father B. will be back."

"You must open it, Andrzej," Tomek said.

Krystyna and Anna had come up from the kitchen to

see the mail. They nodded agreement. "He would want you to read it," Anna said.

Andrzej sighed, stroked his beard, then unfolded the letter and read it aloud: "Your dress is ready." He glanced up. "That's the code for the printing press!" He went back to the message: "ulica Targowa and ulica Różyckiego."

"Warsaw!" Anna exclaimed.

Andrzej finished reading: "Where a bent man in a black hat exits. 15 October. Midnight."

"That's today!" Krystyna whispered.

Andrzej paced in front of Tomek. "The printing press will be sitting there, with no one to pick it up! Father B. has no way of knowing this. There is no one to go get it."

"We must have this press!" Anna insisted.

Calmly, Tomek reached out and took the note from his friend. "I will pick it up."

Andrzej snapped his fingers. "I will help you."

Tomek shook his head. "No. It's too soon for you to risk. Zakopane police will be watching you. I cannot let you do it. Not just for yourself, but for the press."

"Tomek is right," Krystyna said.

Tomek knew that as it was, his future at the university was a distant dream. He would still be a poet. He felt this more deeply than ever. Yet if there were no free press in Poland, if people were forbidden from reading what he wrote, what good could he hope to do?

He smiled to himself. He would do the right thing for Poland and for God, and he had not even paused to ask what Tadeusz would have done.

"*I* will go with Tomek," Anna declared.

Tomek shook his head. "No, Anna. I must go by bus. It will be better if I go alone."

Anna started to protest, but she stopped. Even she had to realize what he said was true. "The risk is great by bus," she said.

"Then Tomek will go by car." Eva was standing in the doorway, her black hair laced with snow. "And I will drive him."

⇥ 22 ⇤

Tomek stared at the slender girl in the doorway, her hair wet and curly from the snow. "You?"

"Yes, me," she answered. "I don't see anyone else around here who can drive. Unless, of course, you're afraid I'll tip off the militia again."

"Eva, I never——," Tomek began.

"We don't have time to argue," Eva interrupted. "We have to get going. I have a reputation for getting lost."

Tomek tried to talk her out of it. It was far too dangerous. He could handle it alone. He tried every argument he could think of, but he was no match for Eva once she'd made up her mind. He had a feeling she didn't lose many fights.

"I'll start digging out the car," Andrzej offered, when it was obvious Tomek had run out of arguments.

"*Boże mój!*" Krystyna ran to Eva and pulled a telegram from her apron pocket. "This came for you, Eva! It is from your father."

Eva ripped off the gray band and read. She nodded, and her eyes misted.

For a minute Tomek feared it was bad news. Then she smiled and tucked the telegram into her pocket. "He's safe. He and Father B. made it to Vienna. Father B. has gone to Rome. But Dad's going to try to get a new visa to come back in."

"What else does he say?" Krystyna asked.

Eva leaned down and hugged Krystyna. "Only that he's safe, Krystyna. He's safe."

Eva stood up, and Tomek could almost see her gather herself. She took a deep breath and let it out. "Well, what are we standing around here for?"

Krystyna made sandwiches, and Anna brought down a blanket to hide the printing press on the drive back.

Tomek helped Andrzej move snow with the broom and a broken spade until they cleared a path to the road. Though snow drifted high in spots, the road looked passable.

Tomek watched Eva as she shook hands with Anna and exchanged kisses on both cheeks with Krystyna. Andrzej stuck out his hand, and Eva shook it, then pulled him in for a bear hug. Tomek could have watched her all day, remembering Eva's way with his parents in Brzegi. "Can I start it?" Andrzej asked.

"Andrzej fixes cars for Father B., but he has not yet driven," Anna explained.

Eva bowed toward the Renault and tossed him the keys. "Be my guest."

Andrzej slid into the driver's seat, leaving the door open and one foot on the ground. He turned the key. Nothing happened. He turned it again. It made a clicking sound, then nothing.

Eva kicked at the frozen rocks around the tires. "It's been sitting too long!"

"I can fix." Andrzej grinned, hopped out of the car, and opened the hood.

Tomek and Eva moved to the front of the car, on either side, as Andrzej peered under the hood. He reached into his pocket and pulled out a handful of thick rubber bands. Humming, he stretched the thickest band around two pieces of metal and flicked it.

"Anna?" he called. "Can you get me a bottle cap?"

"A bottle cap?" Eva repeated.

He grinned up at her. "This is not BMW, Eva."

Tomek had seen Andrzej use a lighted matchstick, a paper clip, and chewing gum to keep Father B.'s vehicles going.

It took the bottle cap, gum, and another rubber band before Andrzej slammed the hood and pronounced, "There."

Eva looked skeptical, but she slid into the driver's seat, and Tomek climbed in next to her. "Here goes," she whispered, turning the key. The engine coughed, whined, then backfired, blackening the snow behind the exhaust pipe. "Andrzej, you're a genius!" she shouted, stopping only to ask Tomek the Polish word for *genius*.

She waved out the open car window. "Don't wait up!"

Andrzej hollered, "One moment!" He dashed behind the car, reached beneath the snow, and came up with a handful of dirt. After rubbing it in his hands, he smeared it over the license plate. "To hide the numbers!" he shouted, rejoining Krystyna and Anna.

Tomek felt a wave of fear, not for himself, but for Eva. "Eva, listen. You should not come. This will be too dangerous. I can still catch the bus if I——"

She cut him off. "Tomek, shut up. You need me and you know it. Besides, it's not just for you. It's for the *dress*."

Tomek knew she was right. His chances of getting the printing press were much better with Eva to drive him. In the past weeks, he'd come to realize that Poland was worth risking his life for. Tadeusz had known this, and understanding his brother's sacrifice at last had brought Tomek a kind of peace. He wanted his country to be free. He wanted to live in a Poland where he could write the poems he desired and people could read them freely. He was willing to sacrifice for this—but not to sacrifice Eva. "Please, Eva?"

Eva tilted her head. "Tomek Muchowiecki, I'm coming. Live with it. Besides, who else would keep you out of trouble?" With one hand on the steering wheel and her other arm over the seat, Eva turned to gaze out the back window. "We're off!" She stepped on the gas. The car lunged forward. "Oops!" She slammed on the brakes, and the engine died.

"What happened?" Tomek asked. He'd trusted Andrzej to fix the car, but it wasn't working right.

Eva sat with both hands on the wheel. "Tomek, do you have your flashlight?"

"Yes, but—"

"Please! We have to hurry!"

Although it was barely afternoon, gray clouds darkened the sky, making it seem more like dusk. Tomek searched in his *torba* for the flashlight he carried everywhere. He handed it to Eva, but she pushed it back at him.

"Shine it there." She pointed to the ball on top of the stick shift.

Tomek directed the light onto the gearshift while Eva studied the diagram etched there. "You don't know how to shift gears?" he asked, worry growing into panic. He should have taken the bus as he had planned. Why had he let Eva have her way?

"Got it! You can turn the light off now."

"Eva? You do know how to drive, right?"

"More or less. I'm just used to automatics."

"So you have your license in America, yes?"

She hesitated. "Well, not exactly."

"What is 'not exactly'?"

"Relax, Tomek! I never met a car I couldn't drive."

The Renault started up again and lunged forward, then slid back, stuck in the snow. Andrzej, Anna, and Krystyna dashed behind the car and pushed until the wheels spun, then caught, and the car chugged out the drive. Eva swerved a little turning onto the road, but she kept inching forward until they were headed up the hill.

"The road should get better," Tomek said as they drove north out of Zakopane. "It is a long drive, perhaps three times as far as Kraków." This was the first time they had been alone since their return from Brzegi. Tomek felt the tension between them like an invisible curtain. Neither of them spoke for a long time.

"Just tell me when to turn," Eva said, clutching the wheel and leaning forward. "Did you ever realize there aren't any streetlights in southern Poland? It's hard to see."

They drove without talking about anything but the route until they were halfway to Kraków. He took advantage of the moments and studied her face, lit by the greenish glow of the speedometer light—her high cheekbones, her tiny chin and full lips. He loved her. In spite of himself, he did.

Snow fell lightly on the windshield, and she turned on the wipers. The *screech, screech* of rubber on glass filled the car. "Do I turn here?"

"Just follow the jog, but stay on this road." Tomek didn't take his gaze off her as they rounded the curve. "Eva," he began, "I never believed you betrayed Andrzej. You must know this." He waited for her to argue. The last thing he wanted was to bring back her anger, but he couldn't rest until he at least tried to make her understand.

"I know."

"You know?"

"You're not that dumb, Tomek."

It was a compliment only Eva could give.

"But you should have spoken up for me," she added.

"You are right," he agreed, angry with himself all over again for his confused silence. "I lack the quick tongue of Americans."

"So you want to start a fight again?" She glanced at him, then back at the road.

He did not want to fight with her. Not now, not ever. "Not for the world, Eva Lott."

"I'm glad," she said quietly.

He reached over and put his hand on her arm. "Eva, when you were angry with me . . ." He sat up straight and made himself continue. "I felt empty . . . as empty as . . ." He struggled for the right word, the hollowness in his soul.

". . . As a Polish meat shop!" She grinned at him. They laughed, draining the tension from the car.

"And I thought *I* was the poet around here." Tomek sat back and stared out at the white flakes caught in the headlight beams. Every inch of metal in the old car rattled as they bounced along the main road.

They rode in comfortable silence for a while. He directed her around Kraków and northeast toward Radom.

"You're going to be a great poet someday, Tomek Muchowiecki," Eva said. "A Polish hero."

Tomek stared at her. It seemed like a lifetime ago when he had stood in line at the university in Łódź, resenting that he could not stay there and study. He had cut himself off from friends, even from family, and convinced himself that Poland's struggle for freedom had nothing to do with him. Now all of that had changed.

"What are you thinking?" she asked.

He started to answer as he always had, to claim he had been thinking nothing. Then he stopped himself. It had been a long time since he'd let anyone, even himself, in on the deepest desires and thoughts of his heart. "I came to Zakopane against my will."

Eva laughed. "Right."

"No one forced me, that is true. But I did not want to come." They had been talking in English up to now, but Tomek didn't want to frame his words, to pause long enough to reframe them from Polish to English. So he continued in Polish, knowing Eva would understand enough.

"When I was a young boy, I idolized my big brother. I wanted to become like him. I would have sacrificed everything, even my life, to win my country's freedom. Then Tadeusz was murdered. And the sacrifice became real, too real."

The car clunked over a pothole, and they both bounced from the seat. Eva glanced at him, her eyes urging him to go on.

"The only reason I came to Zakopane was for the money I'd get interpreting," he admitted.

She glanced at him again. "What changed your mind, Tomek? What happened?"

"*You* happened. Eva Lott happened to me. From the first day I saw you at the Palace of the Kings, screaming at your father"—they both laughed—"I knew I was in for trouble."

Eva faked surprise. "What? You didn't notice my charm and good nature right away?" They were talking in both languages, Eva in English, Tomek in Polish. But it worked well enough.

Tomek laughed. "I thought you were a typical American brat."

"Tomek Muchowiecki, there is nothing *typical* about me!" After a minute, she added, "I never would have guessed you didn't want to be in Zakopane, Tomek." But she didn't sound disappointed in him, more like she was reaching to understand. "When I first met you, I thought you had everything worked out for your entire life. I'd never met anyone so confident, so—"

"Arrogant?"

"Um . . . let's say *sure* of yourself." She smiled at him. He would have climbed the Tatras for that smile.

"I want to be a poet, Eva. But I want to write whatever I want, without fear of censorship. I want the people of Poland to be free, to read whatever they want. And so it seems I cannot have one without the other—poetry and freedom."

They talked as she drove the one-lane road through villages with nothing in them except churches and taverns. Tomek said everything that came to his mind, about Poland, about Tadeusz, about Eva. And she talked, too, about America, her life there, her father, and her mother.

As they passed a co-op farm, the road curved east. Ahead something moved. In the crossed beam of the headlights, Tomek glimpsed a figure. Someone was standing in the road directly ahead of them.

"Eva, look out!" He grabbed the steering wheel. The car swerved. Tall brush rushed at them as they careened off the road, heading straight toward the ditch.

⇥ 23 ⇤

Tires squealed. Snow sprayed the windows. Tomek was sure they were going to crash into the ravine.

Then the car stopped, front tires on the edge of the embankment.

"Why did you grab the wheel?" Eva screamed, breathing hard, leaning over the steering wheel. "You could have killed us!"

Tomek pointed out the window, where a man stood, shaking his fist at them. In his other hand was a bottle. He shouted something, then kept walking, swaggering down the middle of the narrow road.

"I didn't see him," Eva whispered, her voice hoarse. "Tomek, I could have killed him. How could he do that? Walk drunk in the middle of the road, with no streetlights?" Her hands shook.

Tomek covered one of her slender hands with his. "I

should have warned you, Eva. This happens often. Our Communist government raises prices on meat, bread, eggs, all things. Yet they lower the price of vodka. They want to keep us weak, with this false contentment from the bottle. Men who do not feel like men because they cannot afford to feed their families numb themselves with alcohol they *can* afford."

"That's terrible, Tomek."

It was one more thing Tomek determined to change in Poland. "We'd better see if we can get this car back on the road." He pulled out the flashlight again and shined it on the gearshift. "Just in case you want to take another look at *reverse* before we go."

Eva took the flashlight, studied the gearshift, then turned the key. The Renault groaned and sputtered. One rear wheel spun. But the other slowly grabbed enough earth to move them backward and onto the road.

Eva drove even more slowly than before. It was okay. They had time. Tomek didn't want to arrive early and have to wait long in Warsaw.

The rest of the drive they came upon two more drunks in the road. Eva drove around them and lowered her speed even more.

They passed Radom and turned onto the road to Warsaw, still talking about everything, about Poland's history of fighting for independence, about the Soviet control of the East.

"In school we read about the Iron Curtain, but it just sounded like a make-believe, spy thing," Eva admitted.

"On trips to Germany, Father B. has seen the Berlin

Wall," Tomek said. "It is built of concrete and barbed wire, stretching between East and West, guarded on both sides. Two of his friends were shot trying to flee to West Berlin. The wall of Poland is not iron, or concrete, but it is just as strong."

They were quiet for a while. Then Eva said, "Tomek, that wall will come down someday soon. I know it."

By the time they saw the lights of the city, it was almost eleven. Tomek directed Eva to the back roads, skirting Old Town and coming out on the right bank of the Wisła, an old area of Warsaw, known as Praga. They passed very few cars, mostly taxis or city vehicles. The trams had stopped running, and the city, under only a dusting of snow already browned from factory and bus exhaust, seemed unearthly quiet, as if hiding, lying in wait.

"There. There it is," Tomek said. "That is our intersection." The two streets joined in an arc at the top of an old warehouse district. Several abandoned buildings lined the east side of the road, across from an empty lot and what was left of a burned-out house or shop. A single lightbulb strung on a wire, like a telephone wire slung between poles, shed enough light to make out four possible buildings, each with the large entrances apparently boarded up. "I don't know which building it's in."

Eva pulled the car off the road, out of the lighted area. "It's the one the bent man in a black hat comes out of," she said, shutting off the engine. She took a watch out of her coat pocket. With it came the plum pit Tomek's mother had given her. It touched Tomek deeply that she should still have it. She grinned at him and stuck it back in her pocket. Holding the watch to the car window, she said, "We have ten minutes to wait. If anybody drives by, we'll just act like we're necking."

"'Necking'?" Tomek did not recognize this American word.

"Smooching," Eva explained.

Tomek shook his head. "I do not understand 'smooching.'"

"Let me show you." Eva leaned over and kissed him.

He kissed her back, turning in the seat so he could wrap his arms around her the way he'd wanted to do so many times in the past weeks. When they were done, he leaned back. "I like this necking and smooching."

They waited in silence for what seemed like forever, watching each of the four possible doors. The wind blew, shaking the little Renault. The windshield kept fogging over, and they had to rub it off to see.

"What if he doesn't come?" Eva asked.

Tomek shrugged.

She pulled out the watch again. "It's after twelve thirty, Tomek."

Tomek checked in all directions. He knew watchers were everywhere, even on deserted streets.

"Tomek, look!" Eva pointed to the second warehouse. The door moved, then opened a crack.

"Why isn't somebody coming out?" Eva whispered.

"*Shhhh.*" Tomek stared at the door. It cracked open wider. Then out came a thin man, dressed in black, bent over as if leaning into the wind. And on his head was a broad-brimmed black hat.

"That's him!" Eva whispered.

They watched as the man turned and walked away from them. Then they waited until he disappeared into the darkness. Still they sat, not speaking, waiting.

"You think it's safe now?" Eva had her hand on the door handle. "Should we go in?"

Tomek made a silent plea to God that he could say the right thing. "Eva, you need to stay here."

"No way!"

"Please!" He couldn't let her come. He didn't know what was waiting in that warehouse. So many things could go wrong. Grażyna might have gotten word of the meeting and turned them in. She could have set them up. It might all be a trap. And he couldn't risk Eva getting caught in it. "Listen . . ." He chose his words carefully. "We need a lookout here. We don't need both of us in there."

"Then I'll go and—"

"*I* need to go in because we don't know how heavy the printing press is. Honk the horn if you see someone heading in after me. You must be ready to drive away fast."

"Tomek!" Her hand still rested on the door handle, but he knew she was weakening.

"Keep a lookout in all directions." Quickly he opened his door and stepped out of the car. Walking fast, he headed straight to the warehouse, slipped in, and closed the door behind him.

Inside the warehouse the only light broke in through the slats in the door. Tomek reached into his pocket for his flashlight, then remembered. He'd given it to Eva on the road, after the near accident. He shut his eyes, then opened them, trying to adjust to the darkness. He could see shapes around what looked like an empty toolshed. It smelled like grease and decaying flesh. Something scurried in the corner.

There was nothing to do but feel around for the press. He stepped toward a table and felt cobwebs or spiderwebs close around him. Brushing them off his face and arms, he started his search. The printing press could have been anywhere. The room was as large as the basement of Widokówka.

Starting in one corner, he felt under a workbench, checked in boxes against the wall. He didn't even know what to look for. The press could be assembled, or scattered in parts. He moved the length of the room, up and down, getting farther and farther until he reached the opposite wall.

Nothing.

Outside he heard footsteps. Tomek held his breath. The door latch creaked up, and the door was pushed back.

He ducked behind the nearest thing, a tall trash can, and hoped they hadn't seen him. His foot caught. He jerked it away. Something fell, banging on the cement floor, the echo deafening.

"Tomek?" It was Eva's voice.

"Eva! I told you to wait in the car." He stood up, fear draining from him, making his fingers tingle.

"A car drove by, Tomek. I ducked, so I couldn't see. But I'm pretty sure it was militia." A burst of light filled the room, and Tomek could see Eva, holding his flashlight. "So, what exactly does this *dress* of yours look like?"

It took only a minute with the flashlight. In an open

box on a wobbly table sat the printing press, a mound of metal, with loose metal squares piled around the bottom.

Tomek balanced the box in his arms, ignoring his sore ribs and bruised thigh. It was heavy, but he could handle it. He started for the door, when Eva shoved him back. She held her finger to her lips, slid back the door a crack, and peered out. Gasping, she drew herself back inside.

Tomek heard a noise—a car door opening and closing. Then another, followed by the voices of two men speaking Polish. The men exchanged frivolous words as their footsteps drew closer. The box strained against his arms and chest. His fingers slipped, and he lifted his knee to steady his load.

Boots clipped on the walkway outside, not ten meters from them. A beam of light swept the warehouse door. They were making rounds, checking the warehouse district, Tomek thought, praying that the search was not more specific, not intended for them.

Beside him, Tomek felt Eva take hold of the box. She shared his load as the footsteps moved past them. Minutes later, the footsteps returned. Car doors opened, then closed. And the car drove off.

Eva inched toward the warehouse door and peered out again. "Wait here," she whispered. Then before Tomek could stop her, she was gone.

Tomek wanted to run after her. He feared a trap. The militia might even now be lying in wait by the car. Why could Eva not wait for him?

He used his hip to shove the door wide enough to fit through with the box. Outside Tomek stared up the street, but he couldn't see beyond the warehouse to the car, to Eva.

An engine roared. Snow crunched under tires. Tomek half expected to see the militia pull up, their machine guns at the ready. Then he spotted the Renault coming at him. The back door flew open, and the car swerved to the curb.

"Tomek! Get in!" Eva slowed the car, driving one wheel over the curb.

Tomek flung the box through the open back door and jumped in after it, landing on the floor of the backseat, the door open at his feet.

"Close the door!" Eva shouted. "And hang on to your hat!"

⇥ 24 ⇤

Eva had no idea where they were headed as she zigzagged through the streets of Warsaw.

In the distance, she heard the whine of sirens. For all she knew, they could be for her. She made a sharp left turn, then another right, hoping the car wouldn't tip over. "Tomek, are you okay?"

He scrambled up from the floor of the backseat and leaned forward, his head at her shoulder. "Turn up this alley, Eva. And slow down."

She turned.

"Do you think they saw us?" Tomek asked.

"I'm not taking any chances," Eva answered, realizing as she said it that she had never taken more chances than she had in the last hour. She followed the alleyway, glancing at Tomek in the rearview mirror to see for herself that he was in one piece. "You're sure you're all right? Are your ribs okay?"

"I am all right, Eva," he answered. "But we must get out of Warsaw."

She swerved onto a path that led across railway tracks. Behind them, more sirens blared. The car bumped over a series of rails, rolled through a parking lot, and came out on a tiny gravel road. They followed it, staying to the outskirts, far from the lights of Warsaw, until they came to a dead end. Eva slammed on the brakes.

"What do we do now?" she asked, fighting off panic. They were trapped. She couldn't turn the car around and go back, not with police cars cruising Warsaw. Even if the militia didn't know about the press, a Renault with foreign plates, this time of night, had a good chance of being stopped.

Tomek hopped out of the car and climbed into the front seat next to her. "If you can make it up that hill, that is our road right there. I didn't want to risk taking the main connection. You think you can do it?"

It was a short hill but steep as a ski jump. Eva sized it up. She'd only get one try, and it had better be a good one. If she stopped going forward, they'd slide down and probably end up stuck. Picturing the diagram on the gearshift, she put the car in first, aimed at an angle, and floored it.

The car lunged at the hill. She shifted to second. They shot up fast until they were almost to the top. The wheels spun. The rear end shifted sideways. The stench of burning rubber enveloped them.

"Come on!" Eva pumped the gas pedal to the floor and leaned on the steering wheel, as if she could push it up.

They crept forward, then a little more. With a jolt, the Renault lunged, as if leaping over the top of the hill. They bounced on the other side and sped through the ditch and up onto the road. She had to pull hard left to keep from overshooting the road. The car swerved, then straightened on the narrow lane. "Zakopane, here we come!"

Tomek arranged the blanket to cover the box with the printing press. Then he leaned over and kissed Eva on the cheek. "Do not break speed limits. We are not out of woods yet," he warned, checking the road behind them.

Eva knew he was right. The militia didn't need a reason to pull over a car at this hour. They both kept watch as she drove southwest, faster than she'd driven to Warsaw but still not speeding. Each time they met another car, she held her breath until it passed.

They'd been en route about a half hour when Eva heard the wail of a police siren, faint at first, then growing louder. "Tomek," she whispered, as if in danger of being overheard.

"There is a road very near . . . *there!* Take it!" he shouted. "The path, there!"

Eva was on top of the narrow road before she saw it. The siren was getting closer and closer. She swerved the car right, then gunned it and fought to straighten out the steering wheel. Trees lined the bumpy snow-covered road. Tomek reached over and turned off the headlights. "Tomek, I'm going to get us stuck," she cried.

But he wasn't paying attention to her or to the road.

He was turned in his seat, staring behind them into the pitch-black night. "Do you hear that, Eva?" he whispered. "They are going past."

She did hear it. The sirens screamed at an unbearable volume, then faded to a distant drone.

"They are gone, Eva," he said, turning back around in his seat and reaching over to touch her cheek. "You did it."

Eva felt her muscles untangle and her fingers loosen on the steering wheel. She leaned over and kissed Tomek. "*We* did it, Tomek. *We* did it."

Eva had been afraid she'd be too tired to drive all the way back, but now she felt like she could drive forever with Tomek. Once they were back on the road, they both started talking at once. Then they laughed. And before long, they were reliving every minute of their secret mission, going over every detail.

After a while Tomek directed her to another side road that fed into a paved route she recognized. She and Tomek talked about everything, about a free press in Poland, about Tomek's plans to write for the underground publications his brother had talked about. Because Grażyna had betrayed their location in Zakopane, the group would need to find a different village as home base. But they would continue their work.

Then just as suddenly, their mood changed and they were laughing again, as if there were no dangers in the world, only comedy.

"Okay, Eva," Tomek began. "How many militia does it take to change a lightbulb?"

"You're kidding, right?" It was an old joke she'd heard from kids when she was little. Only they'd always asked, "How many Polacks does it take to change a lightbulb?" Back then, she'd never thought of Polacks as people from a real country like Poland.

"It takes thirty," Tomek said, answering himself. "One to hold the ladder. One to hold the bulb. And twenty-eight to fill out the government forms reporting the incident."

She laughed. "The way I heard it was: One to hold the bulb and four to turn the ladder."

"And," Tomek said, "you heard it about Polacks, yes?"

Eva hated to admit he was right, but she nodded.

"We tell all these same jokes on our own secret service, you see? Try this one: What do you call one hundred militia at the bottom of the sea?"

Eva burst out laughing. "A good start! My turn. How do you burn a militia officer's ear?"

It was Tomek's turn to deliver the punch line. "Call him while he's ironing his uniform. How do you burn his other ear?"

Eva had never heard that part of the joke. She shrugged.

"Call him again!"

They rode for a while in silence. It was a good silence, with no pressure to say anything. She thought back to her dates with Matt. Most of the time they had so much fun together. But she could get uncomfortable if they had to drive anywhere very far. She remembered the awkward silences, the times when she'd forced herself to talk through them. Once she'd asked Mel what to do about car conversation, and Mel had told her men liked to talk about themselves. "Get Matt to talk about himself, and he'll think you're the best conversationalist he's ever met." It had worked, too.

But it was different with Tomek. They talked about all kinds of things.

She thought of another joke. "How do you save a drowning militia?"

Tomek didn't answer.

Finally she'd come up with one he hadn't heard. "Take your foot off his head!"

They were still trading jokes long past sunup, when they reached Zakopane. Eva stretched her aching muscles and tapped her toes on the floor. The heater had stopped working halfway home, and her body trembled with cold. All she wanted to do was sleep.

She turned onto their street, then crept down the driveway, parking the Renault behind the house, out of sight.

Eva switched off the ignition and felt the quiet. She smiled over at Tomek. As exhausted as she was, she didn't want to leave this car, this moment, this man. He looked older but more handsome and more vulnerable.

Tomek slipped his hand behind her neck, under her hair. She shivered from his cold fingers, then warmed as he drew her slowly to him. They kissed, long and sweet, as she ran her fingers through his hair and prayed they could always be exactly this way.

Suddenly Tomek jerked away from her.

Eva heard footsteps approaching the car. She looked out the windshield to see Andrzej and Anna running toward them. Tomek scooted away from her.

Andrzej's shirttail hung out. His boots were unlaced. "You are fully *dressed*?" he asked.

For a second Eva thought he'd seen her kissing Tomek. Then she remembered the code word for the press. She climbed out of the car and shook the hand Andrzej offered her. "We did it, Andrzej!"

Anna was already reaching into the backseat with Tomek and helping him pull out the blanket-covered box. The two of them carried it toward the house, and Eva worried that Tomek's shoulder and ribs hurt more than he admitted.

She walked arm in arm with Andrzej as the sun peeked over the Tatras. Eva wished her dad could have been here. This was why he'd come to Poland. She couldn't take her gaze off the mountains and wondered on which snow-capped peak Tadeusz and Łukasz had planted a cross. The sky had an orange tint and shared it with trees, houses, pastures, as if the whole world felt the dawning of a new day in Poland.

⇥ 25 ⇤

Andrzej opened the front door of Widokówka and bowed low to let Eva pass in. Anna and Tomek had already disappeared, probably searching for the best hiding place for the *dress*.

Krystyna came running to greet her. "I have *herbatka* to warm you."

Eva hugged her friend. "Thanks, Krystyna. But all I need is a warm bed."

"I will go help Tomek," Andrzej said, trotting down the steps toward the kitchen.

Krystyna pulled on Eva's arm and led her toward the coatrack. She pointed to a small battered box, half open and held together with string. "It came for you!" Krystyna exclaimed. "All the way from America! Our Polish post was not so kind with it."

The package was from Melanie. Several photographs

peeked out of the ripped side of cardboard. Eva pulled them the rest of the way out and felt herself grinning as she glanced through the pictures. Mel had snapped photos of the swim team waving, of their mall friends holding up a "Miss you, Eva!" sign in front of Abercrombie and Fitch. And there were at least half a dozen pictures of Matt.

Eva slid the string off the box and pulled out a weird-shaped package, wrapped in silver paper. It was heavy and changed shape as she shook it, like a bag full of beads.

She sat on the stairs to unwrap it, while Samson poked his nose in and scratched at the paper. Eva ripped off the paper. Inside was a giant bag of popcorn.

Popcorn! Eva stood up and hugged the plastic bag to her chest. Then she burst out laughing. Samson barked at her.

"Oh, Mel," she murmured. Melanie had no idea what it was like here. What was Eva going to do with five pounds of popcorn? She didn't have a popcorn popper. She didn't even have a real stove.

"It is okay?" Krystyna asked, looking worried.

"It is very okay," Eva answered. Then she had an idea. A wonderful idea. She leaped off the stairs and took Krystyna's hand. "Krystyna, do you know popcorn?"

Krystyna shook her head.

"Popcorn!" Eva repeated. She grabbed the big bag and showed her.

Krystyna touched the bag as if it might contain explosives. "Pope-corn?" she asked.

"Pope-corn. To eat," Eva said, cupping her hand and pantomiming downing a handful of popcorn.

"Eat?" Krystyna asked, studying the tiny rock-hard kernels of popcorn. The expression on her face said she'd like to eat that stuff about as much as Eva would like another chunk of lard.

But Eva wanted to share this gift with her friends. She wanted them to experience popcorn the way she'd experienced Tomek's plum orchard. Or Wawel. Or so many things here.

"Tomek!" she shouted, tucking the bag of popcorn under one arm. She locked arms with Krystyna and hurried down to the basement.

Tomek was feeding coal into the stove. He closed the fire door and turned to Eva. "Is everything all right?"

She joined him by the oven. "Tomek, popcorn. Do you know it?"

"Pope-corn?" Tomek cocked his head to one side.

Perfect! Even Tomek hadn't experienced popcorn. "I'll need the big pot," she said, realizing that she'd never done this without the electric popper. "And a little bit of lard?"

Tomek frowned, but he fetched a small tub of soft, white lard and helped Eva set Pani Kurczak's biggest pot on the stove. As Eva struggled to regulate the heat of the stove's fire, Tomek came up behind her and wrapped his arms around her waist. "So where is your pope-corn?"

She shook the bag and laughed when he made a worse face than Krystyna had. "Don't be afraid of different," she said, throwing his words back at him.

He kissed her forehead.

She dropped a tablespoon of lard into the pot.

Anna came over to investigate. She took one look at the popcorn and made a disgusted sound. *"This* is how we celebrate the arrival of our *dress?"* she asked. "What a waste of lard!"

Anna, Andrzej, and Krystyna sat at the kitchen table while Tomek related the events of the Warsaw adventure.

Eva fed coal into the oven until she felt the heat pour through the burner. It smelled like bacon, and she hoped it would work like oil. The fat sizzled, and she ripped open the popcorn bag and poured all of it into the pan.

Before Eva could put the lid on, Tomek jumped up from the table and peered over her shoulder at the popcorn kernels dancing in the melted fat. "That's it?" he asked. "What should I put on the table?"

"Bowls," Eva said. "And something to drink."

Tomek sighed but started gathering bowls and silverware, and began boiling water for tea.

Tea and popcorn. Who knew?

Eva was alone by the stove when she heard the first kernel pop. It was working! *Pop! Pop! Ping!* The kernels zinged off the metal lid.

Krystyna ran over. "Eva?" she asked, staring at the pot.

Eva laughed. "It's okay," she said. *"Dobrze."*

Wide-eyed, Krystyna backed away.

The familiar popcorn smell spread like earthy incense through the basement. Eva inhaled as if she were bursting out of deep water into fresh air.

The kernels popped fast, the last few raising the flat lid so she could see beautiful white fluffy popcorn. The only thing that could make this moment more perfect would be for her dad and Melanie to be here, too.

Eva set the pan off the stove and removed the lid. Everybody sat quietly at the table, just like they did for meals, while she proudly placed the huge pot on the hot pad in the middle of the table.

At first nobody spoke. Then Krystyna laughed. Nervous laughter traveled around the table.

"What?" Eva asked.

"You pulled a trick!" Andrzej exclaimed. "You must teach me how."

She didn't get it and looked to Tomek for help.

"They do not believe all this white stuff came from that bag of small pebbles," he explained.

"No, it's the same!" Eva said, laughing with them. She'd never thought about how different popcorn looked from kernels. No wonder they didn't think they were the same. It would be like trying to imagine what a plum looked like when you only had the pit.

She picked up one kernel of popcorn, turned it over, and pointed to the little bit of the brown hull still visible. "Popcorn," she said.

They stopped laughing. The room grew still.

Eva took one bowl and scooped it full of popcorn. She set it by her place. When nobody followed suit, she took Krystyna's bowl and scooped it full of popcorn. Then one by one she did the same for the others, filling Tomek's last.

She wished they had salt. Mel would die when she heard they had to eat the popcorn without salt. But since her Polish friends weren't used to adding salt to food, maybe they wouldn't mind.

She took her place on the bench, next to Krystyna, across from Tomek.

Andrzej cleared his throat. She thought of the fan blessing and wondered if Andrzej might be searching his mind for a suitable popcorn blessing.

They bowed their heads, and Tomek reached under the table and took her hand.

Andrzej thanked God for Eva, "our American friend," and whatever she'd made with her hand. Something like that.

Eva gazed around the table. "Come on," she said. "Eat. *Smacznego.*"

Popping a few kernels into her mouth, she muttered, "*Mmmm, dobry* pope-corn."

Nothing. Nobody moved. They kept their hands firmly planted in their laps.

Eva downed a few more kernels.

Nobody budged. They weren't even trying her popcorn. All she wanted was for them to try it. She didn't expect them to love it. Not like she and Mel loved it. Or Dad. But they could try it, couldn't they?

She took one kernel and held it across the table to Tomek. "Open that mouth, Tomek Muchowiecki!"

Krystyna giggled.

Eva focused on Tomek, gazing into his eyes, trying to make him understand that it mattered to her. For whatever reasons, it was important to her that they do this with her.

Tomek opened his mouth and let her drop in the kernel of popcorn. He swallowed, then coughed. Without taking his gaze off Eva, he took a deep breath, picked up his spoon, dipped it into the bowl of popcorn, and came out with a puffy white kernel. He held his spoon in front of him for a moment. Then he brought it to his mouth and ate this one kernel of popcorn.

Around the table, as if on silent cue, Krystyna, then Andrzej, and Anna lifted their hands and spooned dainty mouthfuls of popcorn.

Tomek downed a big spoonful and winked at Eva, reaching for her hand under the table.

Eva held Tomek's hand and watched the others. She knew her friends didn't like the taste. How could they? They'd probably expected it to taste like corn. But they kept spooning.

She watched, and a tear fell from her cheek and landed in her bowl of popcorn. Salt, she thought, grinning. All around her, she heard the crunching of popcorn, the murmurs of polite approval, as spoon after spoon traveled from bowl to mouth.

She grinned at Krystyna. Under the table, Tomek's hand squeezed hers. Then she picked up her own spoon. And in that basement in Zakopane, Poland, Eva and all her friends ate popcorn with their spoons until their bowls were empty.

Eva and Krystyna were washing the last bowl when Andrzej hollered, "Tomek! It's Krzysztof!"

Tomek and Andrzej darted up the steps without another word.

"What's the matter?" Eva asked Krystyna. Her first thought was that the militia had followed them after all, that they were waiting outside to take them away.

"Krzysztof brings your letters," Krystyna explained, touching Eva's arm gently. "Come. We will see if your friend from America has sent us more pope-corn."

They joined Andrzej at the top of the stairs and waited for Tomek to return with whatever Krzysztof had delivered.

They didn't have to wait long. Tomek slipped in, then shut the door behind him. "Eva," he said, handing her a long gray envelope, "I think it is from your father. From Vienna."

Eva tore open the envelope, which bore only her name in pencil, and pulled out a letter and what looked like a train ticket. She read the letter, feeling close to her dad, as if he were there with her, saying the words:

Dearest Eva,

I can only pray that you're safe and well. I am. They're treating me wonderfully here in Vienna. (The food is amazing!) Father B. has gone to Rome in hopes that Wojtyła will be the next pope. I don't tell him how impossible this is, that popes have been Italian for hundreds of years and most likely will stay that way for hundreds more.

More to the point, I have some bad news. At the Austrian embassy, I learned that Polish authorities have listed me as

persona non grata in Czechoslovakia, Poland, Hungary,
Yugoslavia, Bulgaria, East Germany, and Russia. It means
I am denied visas for all of those countries. Talk about
being unwanted! But people here assure me that if I wait
until the end of November and go to a different embassy, I
can get a new Polish tourist visa, no problem. I'll just skip
Czechoslovakia and enter Poland from the north, crossing
the Baltic from Sweden.

Enclosed (hopefully!) you'll find a train ticket to Vienna.
It's too dangerous to have anyone drive you through the
borders. Just leave the car there. I'll need it when I get back.
You should be okay on the train. Sorry. Samson can't come
this trip. I'm sure Krystyna will take good care of him until I
get back. Then I'll bring him with me when I come home.

Once you're in Vienna, you can spend a few days with
me before flying back to Chicago. I've made arrangements
with Melanie's mother for you to stay with them and finish
your senior year. I'd better finish this. The courier is waiting
on me.

I love you, Eva. See you soon! Dad

Eva's head felt foggy. She couldn't clear her thoughts.
Vienna. Chicago. She looked up and saw that they were
all watching her.

"Is it . . . bad news, Eva?" Krystyna asked.

Eva shook her head. She felt light as snow. "Dad's in
Vienna. He wants me to go there. And then to Chicago.
Home."

Andrzej pointed to the ticket that was still in her hand.
"That is train ticket?"

Eva looked inside and tried to read the letters and numbers. *Kraków. Chopin Express. 16 October.*

Anna was reading over her shoulder, fingering the ticket. "Eva, you are leaving tonight!"

Tonight? Eva looked past Krystyna for Tomek. But he wasn't there.

Krystyna and Anna were talking fast to each other. Details were being worked out around her while Eva tried to take it in. But she couldn't think straight. She wanted Tomek. She wanted him to straighten things out.

"The bus will take too long," Krystyna was saying. "Eva drove to Warsaw. She can drive to Kraków."

"She could leave the car with Father Stanisław, the friend of Father B.," Anna suggested.

Eva listened to them as if they were talking about someone else, someone she didn't know.

"Eva, you better get a couple of hours sleep," Krystyna said, putting her arm around Eva and guiding her up the stairs.

Eva heard Samson's toenails clicking on the steps behind them. In a daze she entered her room. Krystyna shut the door.

Eva knew she had to pack. She was going home. Mechanically, she pulled down her only suitcase, then started folding the two shirts she had on hangers, the sweatshirt from Matt, her other pair of jeans.

She started to pack her jogging suit, then folded it and placed it back in the wardrobe, remembering how much Krystyna admired it and knowing she would never take it if Eva just offered it to her.

She should leave the mud boots her dad had picked up for her in Warsaw. They wouldn't exactly go with her school wardrobe at home. Somebody should be able to wear them here. She thought about the day she and her dad had moved into this tiny room and realized they'd have to ship their second suitcases back to the States. All she'd wanted was to crawl into her suitcase and go with it.

Now something inside of her was off kilter. She'd expected to feel nothing short of pure joy when she finally found a way out of Poland. That's what she'd worked for, dreamed of, since the first day she'd set foot on foreign soil. By this time next week, she'd be sitting down to popcorn and pizza with Melanie and Matt.

So why was sadness hanging over her like Polish fog?

Eva picked up Samson and collapsed onto the bed. The room spun when she shut her eyes. Everything was happening so fast. She hugged her dog and thought back to the day of the house blessing, when she'd found Samson in the basement and promised to get them back to civilization. And now she was going.

It didn't seem possible that these were her last hours in Poland.

➻ 26 ⤙

Tomek watched as Eva said her good-byes in the kitchen of Widokówka. He had been surprised when she'd asked him to accompany her to Kraków to the train station. He wasn't sure he wanted to do this. Saying good-bye to Eva Lott would be the hardest thing he had ever done. It might be easier in Zakopane. But it made sense to go with her. At least he could be sure she made the train safely. And he could take the bus back without her.

Eva had slept the few hours since their return from Kraków, but he could not. After the others had gone back to their beds, he had stayed alone downstairs. He had looked through the photographs of Eva's American friends and made himself face the hard truths.

Eva was returning to America, where she belonged—to her friends and to her handsome American boyfriend.

Looking at this Matt's photo was like seeing the American and Swiss athletes on the covers of magazines in the Łódź kiosks. In one picture, Matt was skiing. His goose-feathered jacket must have cost half a year's rent, his boots and denims the other half.

Eva was helping Krystyna pack jelly sandwiches for the train ride. The two exchanged words in low voices, as two old friends. Tomek was surprised how proficient Eva had grown in the language. She didn't speak with perfect Polish, but she could always make herself understood. And she didn't miss much.

"You are very happy to see your friends, Eva, yes?" Krystyna asked, slicing another loaf of dark Polish bread.

"Yeah . . . and Dad. But I'll miss you, Krystyna." Eva's voice shook. "You've been a good friend." She set down bread and knife and hugged Krystyna.

Krystyna didn't speak, but when they let go, her eyes were filled with tears. Tomek looked away. "I will take good care of Samson for you." Krystyna wiped her eyes with the hem of her apron.

They worked their way toward the front door. Tomek picked up Eva's suitcase, remembering his first impression of the American girl with so many clothes in such grand suitcases.

Eva hugged them one by one at the door—Krystyna again, Andrzej, even Anna. "I'll miss all of you." Her beautiful eyes misted over. "I'll write. Thank you for everything!" She picked up Samson and kissed him, then handed him over to Krystyna and hurried outside.

Tomek followed Eva to the car and put the suitcase in the backseat. They moved up the drive and turned onto the street, with Eva staring into the rearview mirror as Andrzej, Anna, and Krystyna waved until they were out of sight. Eva glanced sideways at Tomek, as if about to say something, then stopped.

Tomek felt the iron curtain descend between them.

Neither of them spoke until they were well out of Zakopane. Then Eva said, in Polish, "I will miss the Tatras."

Tomek answered her in Polish. "They will miss you."

Most of the snow had melted or blown away, exposing the fields along the roadside. "You have seen the horses plow this field, yes?" Tomek asked, searching for safe ground so he could at least hear her voice.

She nodded and glanced at the farm.

"The communal farms use tractors. Polish independent farmers still use horses. Their children inherit the land in equal parts, so the farms are as small as a couple of acres eventually. And yet, they have higher production than the big, government farms."

Eva's arms stiffened against the steering wheel. "I'll come back, Tomek." She glanced at him. "After school is over, in the summer, I can come back and stay with Dad at Widokówka . . . or wherever you move to."

Tomek nodded. But he knew she would never come back, not after all she'd been through in Poland. Not with American friends and boyfriend to keep her in her homeland.

He closed his eyes and remembered the drive to Warsaw less than twenty-four hours ago. He could recall every word of their conversation. He had never poured his heart out in this way to anyone.

"We're here, Tomek."

Tomek jerked himself awake, amazed that he'd fallen asleep. How could it have happened? He had such little time left with Eva, and he'd wasted this time sleeping?

Eva parked the car at the church behind the train station and handed Tomek the keys. He would deliver them to the Oasis priest before taking the bus back to Zakopane.

"We have a couple of hours before my train leaves," Eva said, stretching. "Would you mind if I got some souvenirs to take home for my friends?"

Tomek wouldn't have minded if she'd wanted to steal another printing press . . . as long as he could be with her. "We can go to Sukiennice," he suggested, getting out of the car and locking the door. "We can come back for your bag, before your train comes."

They walked through the railway yard, past the Czech Theater and the central Orbis office, or government tourist agency. A winding street opened on to Kraków's central square, a stone plaza with hundreds of pigeons. He wondered what Eva was thinking, what she'd really thought of him the day of Nowa Huta, what she thought of him now.

In the center of the square, they entered the stone archway of shops. Some of them had been there since the Middle Ages.

"I love this part of Kraków," Eva said. "It looks like a postcard." She weaved her way down the long corridor, where craftsmen and tradespeople sold their wares in booths—leather purses, wooden eggs, carved boxes and chess sets, Polish crystal, lace, tapestry, and jewelry.

Content to watch her, Tomek tagged along as she bought three wooden boxes, a chess set, a pair of earrings, a set of carved soldiers, and last, a small tapestry wall-hanging of Wawel.

Eva turned to him. "Could we go see Wawel one more time, Tomek? Or do we need to eat something?"

"I will run and get sandwiches so we may eat *and* visit Wawel," he said. "You must keep the sandwiches Krystyna made for the train. It is a long ride to Vienna." He felt proud that she would want to visit the home of the Polish kings again. It was where he had first seen Eva, her dark hair blowing in the wind as she argued with her father. "I will only be one moment."

Eva watched Tomek race across the square and into a tiny market. She couldn't make herself turn away. How was she ever going to tell him good-bye? Part of her wanted to run away now just so she wouldn't have to. The other part of her wanted to race after him into the store because she couldn't stand missing even one minute of Tomek.

She missed him so much already. He had retreated, and so had she, starting their separation from the minute they'd learned she would be leaving.

A church bell rang, startling Eva so, she almost dropped her sack of souvenirs. She stared at the sack filled with trinkets and Polish wares, as if she could carry Poland home in a plastic bag.

The bells hadn't stopped ringing, and now another

chime broke out from a tower across the square. Then another and another until church bells rang out from every direction.

A woman stumbled out of a shop, wrapping her coat around her as she ran. Then from houses and stores and restaurants all around the square, from every street, people came running. They moved in the same direction, sweeping down on Eva, pulling her in with them. She tried to see over heads to where Tomek had gone. But it was useless, and she gave up struggling and joined the crowd, flowing with them, jostling with children, men in suits, women in street-cleaning orange.

People shouted, but Eva couldn't make out what they were saying over the din of the church bells as continuous as laughter. Cheers burst out spontaneously—cries of joy, she was sure.

Wawel came into view, and Eva used all of her energy to stop and look over her shoulder for Tomek. Someone bumped her from behind. Then the crowd parted around her.

A hand closed around her arm, pulling her sideways through the crowd. She turned and saw Tomek. He shouted something she couldn't understand, as he kept his body between the onrushing crowd and her until they reached the fence.

The courtyard in front of the palace and church was filling with people pouring in from every side. Some of them held candles.

"What is it, Tomek?" she screamed. "What's happened?"

At last he looked at her without glancing away. "Eva,

Father B. was right. Our Polish Cardinal Karol Wojtyła is now Pope John Paul the Second."

Eva stared into Tomek's eyes. It was impossible—a pope who wasn't Italian? A pope from communist Eastern Europe! She threw her arms around Tomek as the crowd broke into a hymn and more and more Poles joined the celebration.

They held hands, pushing into the courtyard, as close as they could get to the church.

"Tomek, won't the militia come?" She remembered the things her father had said about large groups gathering without permission.

Tomek shook his head. "They wouldn't dare. Look at this crowd, Eva."

She gazed slowly at the masses packed into the courtyard, while the bells kept ringing and people kept singing. Tomek was right. There was strength here, and hope, something that refused to be stopped.

They stared together at the faces upon faces of joy. It felt larger than life, bigger than death, a piece of history, a piece of her. Tomek's hand encircled hers, their fingers interlocked. She leaned into him and felt his strength, his hope.

"Eva, it's time."

For a minute she didn't understand. Time for Poland? Time for . . . Then she remembered. Her train departed in less than an hour.

Tomek locked his arm through hers and pushed against the crowd. They were the only ones leaving, and hundreds more were shoving their way inside the courtyard.

Slowly they made it to the gate, then back toward the market square as the crowd thinned.

The markets were almost deserted as they passed, not speaking, on their way back to the train station. The closer they got, the more anxious Eva became. What she felt was a kind of fear, like she'd had when she was a little kid, spending her first overnight at Mel's.

They retrieved her suitcase from the car. Then, since she already had her ticket, they walked straight to the train platforms. Eva hoped the train would be late, but two platforms over stood a train, and above it, a placard that read CHOPIN EXPRESS.

Tomek was staring at it, too, as he held her suitcase with both hands. "It must not be a Polish train," he said. "It is on time. You must walk down those steps and come up on the other platform."

"You're not coming . . . to the train?" Her throat felt dry, and her words sounded as if they'd scraped over sandpaper.

"I will say good-bye here, Eva." He set down her suitcase and shook Eva's hand without looking at her.

Eva let go of his hand and hugged him hard, burying her face in his coat. She didn't want to let him go.

The train whistled. It was the saddest sound Eva had ever heard. In the distance, she could still hear the church bells. Passengers scurried around. The announcer said something over a scratchy speaker.

Tomek gently pushed her away. She looked up and saw his eyes swimming in tears.

Swallowing her own, she grabbed her suitcase and ran

for the platform stairs. She stumbled down a set of steps, then up more steps, coming out on the other side of the train bound for the West, for Vienna, for freedom.

People ran past her on the platform. A crowd had gathered in front of her train.

Eva moved toward the line, feeling trapped, caged, locked in between the trains. Her hand reached into her pocket and closed around the plum pit. She took it out and ran her finger over the curves and edges, studying the lines and holes, the multicolored surface that in a strange way looked beautiful. She could picture Tomek's mother and feel the warmth of her hug, feel it turn into her own mother's hug. She sniffed the plum pit and could smell plum pierogies and hear Papa Muchowiecki's Santa Claus laugh.

She stared at the pit in her fingers. The heart of the plum. The same inside. Beautiful.

It *was* beautiful. So were the Tatras. So was the orchard. The heart of Poland was beautiful! And in that moment, she knew. She couldn't leave this country, not yet. She couldn't leave this man.

The train whistle blew. The conductor shouted for them to board. The whistle blew again, and the train lurched backward, then stopped. Steam billowed out from underneath the belly of the train.

Tomek! She had to catch him before he left the station. Maybe, just maybe, he'd waited for the train to pull out. But the long train, still half in the station, blocked her view of the other platform.

Eva dropped to her stomach and peered under the train.

The platform where she'd left Tomek standing was now crowded with people waiting for their trains. Frantically she scanned the maze of feet until she saw him—Tomek's old boots, the hole in the left toe. But the boots turned and started down the platform.

"Tomek!" she screamed. "Tomek!" Eva jumped up, as if she could make him see her over the train. "Tomek!"

"No one can hear you on the other platform," a white-haired woman said. "Too noisy."

"I have to make him hear me!" Eva explained. "He's leaving!"

The woman breathed in, then shouted, "Tomek!"

Eva shouted with her. Then two boys came over and joined them, yelling out, "Tomek!" A man in a gray suit and another man who looked a little like Tomek's dad joined in, and another woman, and another, until twenty, thirty people were shouting Tomek's name.

Eva turned to them. "Yes! Thank you! Please keep shouting for him."

They did. Their shouts echoed through the train station as, suitcase in tow, she raced down the steps and up the other platform, hoping, praying that she'd be in time.

Tomek had no idea what was happening. It sounded as if the entire Kraków train station were calling his name. He didn't trust his senses. He'd waited for Eva's train to pull out, hoping, praying, for just one more glimpse of her. But the train had boarded, and she was gone.

"Tomek! Tomek!" The shouts came in a myriad of

voices. People on his platform looked at one another and toward the voices on the other side of Eva's departing train.

They had to be shouting for another Tomek. He started to leave, when he heard his name again. This time he knew the voice. "Tomek! Wait!"

Tomek turned to see Eva at the end of the platform. She dropped her suitcase and ran toward him.

He blinked, fearing it was his imagination. "Eva?"

"Tomek!"

"Eva!" He ran as fast as he could toward her. Then he was sweeping her into his arms, holding on so she'd never leave. "You're here. But—"

"Take me home, Tomek. To Zakopane."

"But, Eva, your father—"

"He'll understand. He'll be back soon. And in the meantime, we have plenty to do right here."

The Chopin Express blew its whistle and chugged out of the station. On the platform stood a crowd of people, still yelling Tomek's name. Others waved from the windows of the departing Chopin Express.

"Eva," Tomek asked, still holding her, "who are they?"

Eva waved to the passengers and blew them kisses. "He stayed!" she screamed. "I've got Tomek!"

Applause burst from the platform, in front, behind, and all around them.

Eva threw her arms around Tomek's neck and kissed him, as whistles and applause echoed in the Kraków train station and church bells chimed on the day a Pole became Pope and hope found its way to Poland.

Polish Vocabulary

Amerykański/Amerykanin (m.)	American
Amerykanka (f.)	
bardzo	very much
bigos	a spicy dish made with cabbage and sausage
boże mój	oh my god
centrum	center of the city
co	what
Co to znaczy?	What does it mean?
cześć	hi
dlaczego	why
do widzenia	good-bye
dobry	good
dobry wieczór	good evening
dziękuję	thank you
dzień dobry	good day; good morning
gdzie	where
herbatka/herbata	tea
kawa	coffee

kiedy	when
kto	who
kurczak	chicken
Łapać!	Catch him!
lody	ice cream
mówimy po angielsku	we speak English
nie	no
nie można	you can't do that; impossible
nie rozumiem	I don't understand
nie wolno	not allowed
niedobry	not good
obiad	dinner (the big meal of the day)
osobowy	passenger train
Oświęcim	Auschwitz
pączki	doughnuts
Pan/Pani	Mr./Mrs.
piękny	beautiful
pierogi	stuffed dumpling
piesek	little dog
poproszę o rachunek	check, please
precz z nim	away with him
prędzej	hurry
proszę	you're welcome; excuse me; please
proszę pani	will you please ma'am
przepraszam	excuse me; sorry
przyjaciółka	friend
smacznego	bon appétit; good eating
stać	to stand

tak	yes
tłumacz	translator
toaleta	bathroom
torba	bag
turysta	tourist
tutaj	here
ulica	street
widokówka	postcard
wiem, że to trudne	I know it's difficult
zwariowany	crazy

DAYS

niedziela	Sunday
poniedziałek	Monday
wtorek	Tuesday
środa	Wednesday
czwartek	Thursday
piątek	Friday
sobota	Saturday

NUMBERS

jeden	1
dwa	2
trzy	3
cztery	4
pięć	5
sześć	6
siedem	7
osiem	8
dziewięć	9
dziesięć	10